FATE
THE WINX SAGA

Lighting the Fire

By Sarah Rees Brennan

Scholastic Inc.

Fate: The Winx Saga™ 2022 Rainbow S.p.A. All Rights Reserved.
Fate: The Winx Saga™ is based on the Winx Club Series created by Iginio Straffi.
© Netflix 2022. Used with permission.

ISBN 978-1-338-74498-9

10 9 8 7 6 5 4 3 2 1   22 23 24 25 26

Printed in the U.S.A. 40
First printing 2022

Book design by Katie Fitch

*Dedicated to Anthony and Fionnuala, Lord and Lady
Ardee, and the whole gang, with thanks for the warm welcome at
Killruddery House, the real-life Alfea.*

Fairy Tale #1

The best-endowed, the elect,
All by their youth undone,
All, all, by that inhuman
Bitter glory wrecked.

—W. B. Yeats

Welcome to Alfea!

A pamphlet for prospective students

on our very first Orientation Day

The castle of Alfea was built long ago as a place dedicated to educating young fairies and encouraging the spirit of community between those who possess different fairy magics. A hundred years later, the Specialists' Hall was added, the military division where those who are not fairies—but who are our allies—can be trained in the arts of war.

Whether you are a Specialist or a fairy, whether your fairy magic is water, earth, light, mind, technology, fire, or air, today we welcome you to join this ancient tradition! Walk the grounds of Alfea, discover the maze, ramble through the woods (please do not get too close to the Barrier), and begin your journey of self-discovery within these timeless stone halls.

SAFETY NOTICE:

- Don't venture near the East Wing, as it is in a state of disrepair.

- Don't touch any of the plants in the greenhouse without Professor Harvey's direct supervision. Many of these plants are magical or poisonous. Or magically poisonous.

- Don't ask a Specialist to fight with you, as they may take your head clean off.

- Don't underestimate magics you are not familiar with. You may be an Earth Fairy, able to command all growing things in the ground, but a Water Fairy can drown you, and a Light Fairy can blind you. Remember, it's important to stay respectful of others. Our vision for Alfea is harmony among all.

THIS SECTION IS FOR FIRST WORLD FAIRIES
AND CHANGELINGS ONLY. FEEL FREE TO SKIP IF
YOU ARE FROM SOLARIA, ERAKLYON, ETC.

This realm must seem very different to those of you from the human world, with magic instead of electricity, and powerful kings and queens instead of presidents and prime ministers. Let me assure you of the first question everybody asks—we do have the internet. Though it isn't powered like your internet, you can connect, and your phones will work here. You can even call home!

THE HEART
GROWS OLD

I n the fairy realm of Solaria, by the waterfall and the
woods, stood a castle. Every fairy with sense sent their
children to Alfea, the only educational facility in all
the realms that turned out model fairy citizens.

Farah Dowling, headmistress of Alfea, took great pride
in that reputation. She'd sacrificed enough to uphold it. She
wouldn't let anything harm it now.

Her pride in Alfea was why she'd decided to host this
Orientation Day, perhaps against her better judgment. She
considered the page before her and crossed out the words
"and changelings" because really, they were enlightened and
modern fairies. Changelings didn't happen in this day and age!
Then she put down her draft of the "Welcome to Alfea" pamphlet for Orientation Day and slid out the secret letter beneath
so she could give it one last look.

Usually, she let her assistant handle the paperwork. She'd hired a human assistant because she wanted to show people humans and fairies working together in harmony, but it had emerged that Callum wasn't good for much besides keeping the filing in order. Farah wasn't sure what to do with her secretary. He had somewhat of a chip on his shoulder.

She knew one thing. Callum wasn't allowed near this letter. Nobody else could see it. When it came to records on Rosalind, the former headmistress of Alfea, Farah Dowling took matters into her own hands.

She had carefully hidden all traces of Rosalind, but evil had a long, strange harvest. Farah could toil every day for years doing good deeds, wiping out the stain of what had come before. Yet the old darkness lay beneath every surface she tried to clean. Sooner or later, it found its way through the cracks in the facade and spread like oil.

This time evil had come in the form of a scrawled note of Rosalind's, unaddressed and apparently never sent, tucked away in a book of magic long left unopened. Today, Farah had slid out the paper, yellowed with the passage of sixteen years, and felt her heart jolt on recognizing the writing. She'd received so many commands written in Rosalind's spidery, forceful hand. She had killed on Rosalind's orders, back when she was young and a soldier. Even now, Rosalind's words made Farah want to spring into action.

She had sneaked away early this morning and, by flickering torchlight, pored over the letter alone in the abandoned

East Wing. Rosalind's language was cryptic, but Farah knew how to decipher her meaning. Rosalind hinted at something precious hidden in the First World, that strange land where the humans lived and electricity served instead of magic. Knowing Rosalind, whatever she treasured must be either a magical prize or a terrible weapon.

Perhaps both.

After careful study of the directions in the letter, Farah had retraced Rosalind's long-ago steps, and narrowed her search down to a place with the bizarre name of California. Then she had asked a friend for help with tracing magic— and gone back to work with the guilty secret like a stone weighing on her chest.

Now Farah stood at her desk, stowed the scrawled paper away, and walked out into the halls of Alfea. The heels of her sensible, laced shoes echoed against the stone, and her hands were shoved deep in the pockets of her trench coat. The students scattered as they heard her coming, their laughter lingering behind them.

Farah had never been the warm and fuzzy type. She'd set up this Orientation Day because she knew that when she showed parents and students around the school, she seemed distant, and she wanted everyone to feel welcome here. If she invited all the potential students to their school at once and gave everyone a chance to mingle, it might be easier.

Sometimes, as she watched students racing around Alfea, Farah was sorry for her natural reserve. Farah had mastered many fairy magics, but she'd been born a Mind Fairy, a rarer kind of magic that could discern feelings and dip into thoughts. People seldom wished to be close to Mind Fairies, and it could hurt Mind Fairies to be close to them. Long ago, Farah had learned to keep her distance to protect herself and others. No matter how lonely that could be sometimes, it was a lesson she'd never been able to forget.

Farah looked around Alfea with the affection she didn't know how to show her students. Water Fairies with their magic manifesting in shimmering blue droplets. Air Fairies making their atmosphere vibrate. Earth Fairies filling the world with fruit and flowers. Light Fairies illuminating the sky. And Fire Fairies with the power to warm any hearth. Fairies with other, rarer powers, too. And the Specialists, Silva's charges, who protected all the rest. She understood why Rosalind had collected protégés. If any one of those bright creatures ever felt the urge to come to her, Farah would teach them all she knew.

Only she didn't want to be like Rosalind, to lure students in and use them, and she didn't know Rosalind's trick of winning followers to her side. So Farah maintained her distance, and smiled to herself as the students ran by.

Once she had been as young as they were now. They had all been young, her friends who loved one another with bonds forged in battle. Two fairies and two Specialists: Farah Dowling and Ben Harvey, and Saúl Silva and Andreas of Eraklyon. But Farah and those dear friends had never had the chance to be truly young. They had been a team of elite soldiers, trained to be ruthless in the elimination of evil. Their leader Rosalind had made certain that they were iron.

At the time, Farah had been proud to serve. She hadn't questioned Rosalind's training until it was too late.

Now her nightmares were not about the monsters she had fought, but the monstrous deeds she'd done. Now Farah's only goal was that the students of Alfea never become what she'd become.

She wondered if she should tell Saúl or Ben where she was going. Perhaps she should ask one of them to come with her. She emerged from the carved oak doors of the school and looked down the tree-lined avenue, to the twin lakes where the Specialist students learned the art of war from the best soldier Farah knew.

Saúl Silva stood, arms crossed and blue eyes narrowed, watching a pair of students spar. One student was clearly winning. Farah recognized Sky's fair hair, but she would have known who it was by Silva's face alone. To an outsider, Silva might only look stern, but he'd been her comrade for a long time. Farah could see the pride on his face as he watched the boy he'd brought up.

She could do this alone. She shouldn't bother Saúl.

She wasn't like her old friends. Andreas was dead and past needing anything. Ben had his children to love. Saúl had Sky, Andreas's child, to protect.

What Farah had was Alfea. She had both no children and many children. She was responsible for every soul in Alfea, from their haughty young princess to the humblest fairy. She would never let anything touch the golden youths of this new generation.

Whatever weapon or treasure Rosalind had hidden in the First World, Farah would find it, and destroy it, and come back in time to conduct the orientation celebrations without a hitch. Farah would do whatever it took to make sure every soul in Alfea stayed safe, and happy, and innocent.

SPECIALIST

Alfea was the worst place in the world, and Riven was miserable. The only thing he was learning at school was how to get his ass kicked, and he'd learned this lesson long ago. He felt he was ready for his PhD in being a total loser. "Wow, Dr. Riven," future losers would say. "You've truly made failure an art form. Inspiring. I can't wait to read your flop thesis."

It was nineteen minutes until the end of class.

Riven faced his sparring partner bravely for approximately one second and then dodged the strike of Sky's staff, hitting the platform hard with his shoulder. Sky laughed heartlessly and beckoned Riven to his feet, not even breathing hard. Riven gritted his teeth. Sky thought he was so much better than Riven, just because . . . he was so much better than Riven.

The spring air still had a bite to it, ruffling the dark surface of the lakes their sparring platforms were suspended on. Tender new leaves rustled on the oaks and the copper beeches, stretching massive branches above their heads. Riven was freezing in his sleeveless Specialist uniform. He cast a yearning look toward the benches on the bank, where he'd left his nice warm hoodie and his cool leather jacket.

"Keep at it!" barked Specialist Headmaster Silva. "Never admit defeat!"

But all Riven wanted to do was admit defeat! *Yeah, Sky, you can kick my ass. Yeah, you can do it over and over. Do I even need to be here for my humiliating defeats any longer? Can't I just carve my face on a log, you tip the log over, and then we call this done?* All the other Specialist students could point and laugh at Log Riven, and Riven could go for a nature walk.

Sky's staff connected with Riven's, hard enough to send a jolt through the bones of both Riven's arms. No nature walks for Riven.

Riven didn't understand how the novelty wasn't wearing off. Like, was Sky not bored? Riven was bored.

It was fifteen minutes until the end of class.

When Riven had come to Alfea at the start of the year, he'd self-consciously hoped his roommate would be cool. Riven wasn't the Mr. Popular type, but he'd envisioned having a small gang of friends to hang out and judge others with.

Once he actually saw his roommate, Riven realized his wish had been granted and his fairy godmother had actually gone way too hard on this one. His roommate was much too cool. *Abort. Abort.*

He'd seen Sky around, at military contests and training for Specialist hopefuls. They knew each other well enough to nod to when Sky went past to collect medals. Riven hadn't felt good about the Sky situation from the first moment, when Riven saw Sky's heroic jawline and fancy hair. But at Alfea, Riven was stuck with Mr. Hero, and he decided to make the best of it. Sky seemed nice enough, so Riven thought maybe they could make being roommates work. Possibly even be friends. Riven and Sky stood together awkwardly during the welcome party and watched a blonde in a glittery power suit ordering around her fellow students as if they were her minions.

"Heh," said Riven. "Get a load of her. What a princess."

Sky gave him a funny look. "She *is* a princess," he said.

"How do you mean?"

"I mean," said Sky, "she's the daughter of Queen Luna. The ruler of Solaria?"

11

"Oh," mumbled Riven.

Sky coughed. "And, uh. She's my girlfriend."

"I'm gonna stand over there now," announced Riven, and went over to a stone archway where there were some interesting vines. He communed with the vines for a solid hour.

Sky went over to join Princess Unbearable, whose name was apparently Stella. The princess laid her hand upon Sky's arm and beamed around the courtyard, her pride of possession shining as bright as the magic lights dancing around her glossy blonde head.

So the party was a bust.

Then during their very first lesson, Specialist Headmaster Silva—a man with terrifyingly direct blue eyes that never blinked—told Sky and Riven to spar and hold nothing back so he could evaluate their skills.

Sky gave Riven two black eyes and sprained Riven's ankle. Headmaster Silva said that Riven had actually sprained his own ankle in his rush to escape, but the black eyes were definitely Sky's fault. By the end of the first class on their first day, everyone had Riven's number, and it was real low.

To do him justice, Sky apologized that night after lights-out, although he'd laughed while he did so—as if he found sprained ankles hilarious.

Riven was still trying to get on with his roommate, so he waved a hand dismissively. "It's whatever. I'm not that into this whole soldier-boy thing, anyway. Nobody ever asked me if I actually wanted to be a Specialist."

Sky seemed lost.

"Swords are cool," Riven elaborated, "but the whole idea of perishing to protect the realms is a lot. Like, what have the realms ever done for me, exist? Wow, guess I'll die. And what does it matter if you go out like a chump, or like Andreas of Eraklyon? You're still stone-cold dead."

Sky stared at him blankly. "Andreas of Eraklyon?"

Riven was pleased that his perfect roommate didn't know everything, after all. Andreas of Eraklyon was practically a poster boy for Specialists, a hero of the war with the Burned Ones a generation ago.

"C'mon, you must have heard of the dude. Soldier who led forces against the Burned Ones, those creepy monsters we used to have hanging around the place. Andreas is very famous. Also very dead."

"I have heard of him. He was my father," said Sky.

"Argh," murmured Riven. "Well, that's incredibly awkward."

Sky nodded, hero jawline tight. Right, he'd probably inherited the jawline.

"What do you say I put my head under this blanket," Riven suggested slowly, "and I just don't come out all year?"

"Okay," said Sky.

Riven pulled the blanket over his own face and stared despairingly at the darkness.

That put the last nail in the coffin of getting along with his roommate. Riven was counting the days until his

13

first year was over and he could room with someone else. Anybody would do.

Until that happy day of release, Headmaster Silva appeared to have decided Sky and Riven were a matched set, and he paired them up to spar together every day. The sparring sessions seemed endless, but now the end was nigh. It was so nigh Riven could taste it.

One minute until the end of class!

Sky struck and Riven managed to dodge. Another session with no black eye, *score*.

"You're really getting—" Sky began.

"Would you look at the time? It's get-the-hell-out o'clock already!" said Riven, and got the hell out. He went rolling lightly off the platform, down the bank, and away from Sky, the training platforms, the Specialist headmaster, and the Specialists' Hall.

He hated the whole landscape. The airy mountains, the rushy glen, the high hilltops ringed with white mist. The fairy realms where soldiers had once stalked monsters, swords cold silver in the woods and beneath the pale moonlight. Silva was trying to make them into troops who would all charge into battle together without question, killers fashioned to fight a war long over. Riven would never be like those warriors who had gone a-hunting.

He hated every building and every person in Alfea. Except one.

He was almost gone, when Headmaster Silva snapped, "Riven. Wait."

LIGHT

Alfea was the best place in the world, and Stella had never been happier.

She could admit now she'd been slightly nervous before coming to Alfea, but she should have known this was where she belonged. This was the place where she would learn to be the powerful woman she was destined to become. She had to rule a school before she could rule a kingdom.

"Ladies," Stella announced to her suitemates. "That's a record. Five minutes and my homework is done."

She spread her hands expressively and a light show flared to life, surrounding her face in a frame so it seemed as though Stella was the center of a magic mirror.

Ricki and Ilaria clapped for her, and Stella spun in a circle, allowing herself a moment of smugness. Well, maybe more than a moment. *Don't hide your light magic under a bushel*, her mother said often. The point was to always impress people, but never seem as though you were trying to impress them.

Stella had always tried very hard. These days she was

finally succeeding. As soon as she'd come to Alfea, people had crowded around her as if . . . as if she were Queen Luna herself.

The princess was well named, courtiers back home flattered. *She is a bright star, but she could never compare with the sun that is her mother.*

If people were talking about names, they should know her mother's name didn't mean *sun.* It meant *moon,* and moons reflected light. All their brightness was stolen.

Stella didn't want to be a star. Stars lived in the dark, and she was out of the dark now. After years of being outshone, she was the brightest thing in the sky of Alfea.

"This leaves me with two hours to select the perfect date outfit," Stella continued. There were so many choices. Even before she picked clothes, she had to choose between a high pony and relaxed curls, or potentially a braid. And then there was the question of hair clips versus hair bands.

Stella used her magical ring often, to go to the human world and attend Fashion Week, but right now she liked it here at Alfea better than anywhere else.

Ricki laughed. "As though you have any outfits that aren't perfect."

"My man likes to see more skin than you usually show, Princess," said Ilaria, then relenting, "but you do always look fabulous."

Sky, unlike Ilaria's boyfriend, Matt, would never mention wanting to see more skin. Sky was a gentleman. Stella let an eyebrow flick up. "You know it."

Don't let anyone steal your power, her mother said, then added, *But only choose those who enhance it.*

For your first year, you were randomly assigned roommates, and either given a suite with roommates or a bedroom with a single roommate. Stella had been put in one of the suites at Alfea: five girls, three bedrooms, and a common room. Since Stella was the princess, naturally she got the single room. Their suite was on the topmost floor, so Stella had the closest thing to a tower room at Alfea. Stella had the walls painted blue, set up several mirrors to catch all her angles, and affixed pictures of herself with all her fun, new friends to the wall with sparkles of light.

Sometimes when she woke up in the dark, shivering and afraid, with the wind whistling past the tower window, Stella wished she had a roommate in there with her. During the day, she was happy to get special treatment.

The arrangement suited Stella well enough for now, but in second year you were allowed to pick your own roommates. If your best friend didn't want to share with you, then you didn't have a best friend. Stella had to make a choice.

The problem was, Stella wasn't sure who to pick.

If it was down to who Stella liked more, that was Ricki.

Spending time with Ricki was always fun and oddly relaxing. Ricki was a blast, and she'd never said a single mean thing to Stella.

That was the problem. Sometimes a girl had to be mean. Besides, being nasty meant you had enough social standing to get away with being nasty. Ilaria certainly knew how to be mean, and she was dating one of the second-year Specialists. Ricki wasn't seeing anyone. It was better to be part of a power couple. Stella was keenly aware that her mother would have picked Ilaria for Stella's friend without a second thought. The fact that Stella wanted Ricki instead was more proof that Stella was pathetic and weak.

Stella glanced out her tower window in the room that had been decorated to be fit for a princess, her eyes lingering on dark waters and bright hair. Beyond the castle courtyard lay the Specialists' lakes, where her boyfriend had finished winning another victory.

She loved Sky. He was the world's greatest accessory, better than any bag or jewelry. All the other girls were jealous Stella had him. Even her mother thought Stella's boyfriend was worthy of a princess.

And Stella never forgot that Sky had seen her, even when her mother's radiance made Stella all but invisible. Sky had wanted to protect her.

Only at Alfea, Stella didn't need protection anymore.

It made her feel guilty to admit it, but sometimes Stella thought that she'd rather hang out with Ricki, Ilaria, and her other suitemates than with Sky. She had so much in common with her friends. Once, when Sky had arrived to pick her up, the girls barricaded the double doors and made him wait because they were having so much fun. Sometimes it seemed as if getting ready for dates was more fun than the dates themselves.

That was only natural, Stella told herself hastily whenever that treacherous thought crossed her mind. She'd known Sky for so long; of course new people and surroundings were exciting. After so many years wanting more, it was thrilling to have everything. Now she had the best friends and the best boyfriend. After so long in the cold dark of someone else's shadow, she was the star of the school.

"Show us the first outfit," suggested Ricki. "I can't wait to see."

Stella turned to face her friends, though she kept watch on her reflection out of the corner of her eye. It was her policy to keep reinforcing her natural lighting with magic, replenishing her glamour every time it faltered. Who said you couldn't live real life with filters? Stella refused to accept the premise of the term *Instagram worthy*: Instagram should be worthy of *her*. Instagram needed to get on Stella's level.

Ilaria's eyes were envious as she watched Stella. Ricki smiled as though honestly enjoying the show, and Stella made up her mind. She could transform Ricki into the ideal roommate. She was the princess—she should have whatever she wanted. Stella had a plan, and later Sky would help her with it.

All Stella had to do was keep shining and everything would be perfect.

EARTH

Alfea was the best place in the world, and her father, Professor Harvey, was the best teacher in the world. If Terra could just be a student at Alfea already, she would achieve perfect happiness and have nothing more to ask from life.

But she still had to wait one more year before she was old enough, and this year was the worst. Before, she'd always had her brother.

Terra and Sam Harvey had grown up at Alfea because they were the professor's kids. Her dad said Headmistress Dowling and Headmaster Silva couldn't do without him. She was raised in the knowledge that someday her home would be her school. All her life, Terra had lived side by side with the students of Alfea, as though they were rare plants under glass in her father's greenhouse. She could admire them, but she wasn't allowed to come close.

At first the students seemed so much older and cooler, it didn't matter. Terra knew she'd get to go to Alfea someday.

But recently, she'd started longing for someday to bloom into today. She wanted to walk among the chattering groups of friends, to be part of what she'd always admired. She wanted that so badly, it was starting to hurt.

Sam and Terra were a pair, like peas in a pod. They had to be close, because they didn't have anyone else. Terra had always hoped her beautiful cousin Flora would visit, but year after year had passed, Terra had waited, and Flora hadn't come yet.

Sometimes Sky was at the castle, too, though Sky lived in the Specialists' Hall when he was there. Sky was Sam's age so it would be reasonable if they were friends, but Sky was always with Specialist Headmaster Silva, who was a completely terrifying person. Even more terrifying than Silva was the legend of Sky's father, a famous hero and martyr.

Sam and Terra figured Sky thought he was better than they were. When Headmaster Silva went on missions or to visit the queen, Sky went with him. Sky had dated Princess Stella practically since birth. Sky was so polite that it was a wall: a charm obstacle rather than a charm offensive. Once Sky had suggested that Sam practice the sword with him, and seemed startled when Sam said he didn't want to be cut in half, thanks.

You couldn't even be mad at Sky. Obviously, he had better things to do than mess around in the dirt of the greenhouse with a grubby brother-and-sister pair who cared more about composting than the crown jewels.

Terra had Sam, so she was never lonely. Until this year, when Sam started at Alfea. Her brother became one of that vivid, glamorous crowd of students and left Terra far behind.

At first, Terra showed up after class, hoping Sam would introduce her to his new friends. She believed she could make friends with them, too, and it'd be just like she was going to Alfea a little early. Next year, she told herself, the kids in Terra's year would be so impressed she had all these older friends.

Except when Terra turned up outside his classroom door, Sam pretended not to see her. And Terra didn't even get the hint then. Terra wasn't great at getting hints. Sam had to spell it out for her.

"Quit bugging me, Terra," Sam had snapped on the third day. "How am I ever going to make any friends if my little sister is stalking me?"

"Yeah. Roll away, butterball," whispered an Air Fairy who looked as though she weighed about as much as air, and giggled.

Terra was *almost* sure Sam hadn't heard that. She wished she was completely sure. Whether he'd heard or not, Sam had turned away and had left Terra standing in the hallway alone. A butterball in a chunky floral cardigan, with no friends and no classes to attend. She didn't belong at Alfea yet, and she didn't belong with her brother any longer.

Her only comfort was the greenhouse.

Terra sighed, arm propped on one of the black lab tables where she made potions and distilled oils. She glanced at the crate in the corner and then looked at the clock. She was extremely tempted to open the lid and take a look. Just a teensy peek.

But no! She should wait.

Only it seemed her whole life was waiting these days. Terra hesitated.

The door of the greenhouse swung open. Headmistress Dowling stood framed among the winding vines. Terra sat up straight so fast, she almost fell backward off her stool.

"Ms. Dowling!" she exclaimed. "What a surprise! You never come here. I mean, of course you can come here anytime you like. You're always welcome. And you're the headmistress. Which you know."

Terra took a deep breath and held it, counting to five as she did so. Her annoying brother had advised her to do that when she really got going.

"Is your father here, Terra?" Ms. Dowling asked.

Terra let out her breath. "Oh, my dad. Of course, you want him. He's your right-hand man! Well, I guess Mr. Silva's your right-hand man. My dad's your left-hand man, I suppose you'd say. Would you say that?"

Ms. Dowling stared at her. Ms. Dowling's brown eyes were warm, but her stare was somehow chilling. Terra wondered how she managed that.

"Dad's on a nature walk near the Barrier with the second years," Terra told Ms. Dowling hastily.

"Ah," said Ms. Dowling. "When he returns, will you give him this?"

She laid a note down on the lab table, a cream-colored envelope with *Ben* written on it in Ms. Dowling's firm handwriting. Terra was instantly worried. Ms. Dowling almost never called her dad "Ben." It was always "Professor Harvey." If Ms. Dowling was distracted enough to write *Ben* . . .

"Thank you, Terra," said Ms. Dowling, and turned around, shutting the door with a slam.

Ms. Dowling was a cool and efficient lady, and she'd never really been a people person, but she seemed more extra than usual today. And Terra was tired of waiting around. She jumped up and crept out of the greenhouse, sticking close to the wall as Ms. Dowling walked down the path along the lawn into the woods.

Terra knew every inch of the grounds at Alfea. She watched Ms. Dowling's progress with puzzlement.

Ms. Dowling didn't go near the shimmering blue of the Barrier that protected them from monsters that had been defeated a generation ago, or near the barn where Terra's dad had once cared for an injured fairy steed. Terra had been forced to follow her dad then, but secretly bring treats and ointments later, because it was a pony! Terra loved ponies. It was okay to break rules for love.

Now she was following Ms. Dowling, who headed for the overgrown garden by the woods. There was so much ivy heaped on the walled garden that the walls looked green.

Ms. Dowling's head swung around suddenly. Terra's heart jumped into her mouth. She flattened herself against the wall and sent out tendrils of magic, small as sprouts, asking the ivy to veil her from sight. The ivy obliged, settling around Terra's shoulders and her hair in an embracing mantle.

Seeing nobody, Ms. Dowling's air of tension faded away, replaced by her usual cool confidence. She stepped unerringly up to a spot that looked like just another piece in the dark green wall, and her dark eyes flashed silver. Ms. Dowling was such a powerful fairy; she could control many of the elements, whereas most fairies only had power over the element they were born to.

The ivy lifted to show the crumbling arch of a doorway. Ms. Dowling stepped through, and the leaves fell back as though the imposing figure of the headmistress had never been there.

Terra stepped out from her cloaking ivy and moved toward the hidden doorway, hand out, but then she considered the time and bit her lip. She shouldn't snoop in Ms. Dowling's business, anyway. There was unlikely to be a pony in need on this occasion.

She didn't want to miss the sunset. Terra turned and ran back to the castle.

SPECIALIST

"Hang back for a second," said Headmaster Silva. "Let's change up your partner, Riven."

The words Riven had been longing all year to hear. Maybe he could spar with Kat—she was cool. His eyes went to Kat's cloud of dark hair, and then he reconsidered. Kat was the youngest Specialist in their year, and one of the best. But she hadn't liked Riven since Riven tried to avoid Sky by hanging out with Kat and a cute friend of hers, not realizing until far too late that he was actually crashing a date between Kat and her girlfriend. Kat was vicious and skilled. Riven wanted a fight he could win.

Silva clicked his fingers. Every movement the man made was like a decisive door slam. "Mikey, you're up."

He was indeed. Riven's eyes traveled up. And up and up.

"Hey, Mikey," Riven said. "Where's your staff?"

Mikey grunted. "I just punch people."

Was this a murder attempt? What had Riven ever done to Silva? Maybe Silva just wanted his precious Sky to have a single room.

Riven attempted to preserve *his* precious life. "It's the end of class—"

"Quick bout." Silva clapped his hands together.

Sky hovered attentively at Silva's elbow to watch and learn from Riven's tragic demise. Sky was already taller than Silva, Riven assumed because of his hero genes. Sky wasn't taller than Mikey. Riven was pretty sure there were nearby cliffs that were shorter than Mikey.

Mikey punched in the direction of Riven's head, and Riven dodged for his life.

"Good!" said Silva. "Keep moving."

Why was Silva testing him like this? *Headmaster Silva, my guy,* Riven thought. *I'm literally not one of your strongest soldiers!* He wouldn't hesitate to throw himself into the lake and wait there, breathing through a hollow reed, until everybody went away.

Except people were watching. The same students who'd sniggered and called him pathetic for spraining his ankle. Riven wanted to be a cool rebel loner, not a tragic nerd shunned by the population.

Riven dodged another punch and resisted the urge to jump in the lake. He was used to sparring with Sky by now. Mikey wasn't as fast as Sky, at least.

"Use your speed, Riven," commanded Silva.

What did Silva think he was doing, exactly?!

"Use your strength, Mikey," barked Silva.

Right, he'd almost forgotten that Silva was plotting his murder. Riven took another look at the flesh sledge-hammers that were Mikey's fists and flinched.

"Don't hesitate," advised Sky, as if he was a teacher.

"Don't *patronize* me," snapped Riven, turning his head.

In the split second it took for Riven to turn his head, Mikey's fist connected. It hurt just as much as Riven had thought it might, and also sent Riven staggering off the platform and into the lake.

He rose from the lake, literally spitting mad. Also spitting out duckweed.

When he blinked water out of his eyes, Headmaster Silva was shaking his head. "You're disappointing me, Riven."

You're a sadist, sir. Riven thought of the time he was losing right now, thought about where he wanted to be. He scrubbed pond scum off his face and didn't say it.

"Can I go now?"

Silva sighed and nodded. Riven seized his cool leather jacket and ran, away from the lakes, down the path, and past the arrow-slit windows and glass dome of the Specialists' Hall.

On the way he saw Headmistress Dowling's assistant, Callum, not on the path but slinking from tree to tree.

Riven only saw him because he paid attention to trees. Was Callum on some sad nature walk for one?

Wasn't like Riven could judge.

He shrugged to himself and raced on.

SPECIALIST

"Your friend Riven needs to have a breakthrough, and soon," said Silva. "I'm tired of watching him choke."

Sky made a face. "Yeah, that wasn't great."

The other Specialists had all trickled back to the hall as light ebbed from the sky. Riven had run out of class as though he was on fire, when, in fact, he'd got his ass dumped in the lake. It was just Sky and Silva now, the way Sky liked it best.

But Silva was frowning, and that always made Sky's heart sink. "You've been insisting on training with him all year, but he's not getting any better. You should diversify to keep up your skill levels."

Sky wasn't ready to give up on Riven yet. But he didn't argue with Silva. He never did that. He nodded instead.

Silva's frown turned thoughtful. "The problem is, none of them are at your level. You're head and shoulders above the rest."

Sky knew he was. He'd worked hard to be the best. To make Silva proud of him.

Sky waited, in case Silva maybe wanted to say he was proud of Sky. Silva didn't. That was fine, though: It was understood between them.

"I'll get some of the Specialist teams to come into the school for this Orientation Day of Farah's and give demonstrations," Silva decided out loud.

Sky hesitated. "So . . . I'll just keep sparring with Riven until then?"

Silva gave a curt nod. Sky was relieved.

He hadn't spent a ton of time with people his own age, except for Stella. He was always with Silva, receiving the world's most personal army training. Sky was ready to be an army of one and live up to his father's legacy. He knew Silva had raised him for that purpose.

It was just that . . .

It got lonely, being an army of one.

He'd tried to befriend Sam Harvey, Professor Harvey's son, by offering to teach him swordwork once. Sam and Sam's little sister gave Sky matching appalled stares, and Sky politely receded. It was for the best, anyway. He figured he'd have more in common with a Specialist. Another Specialist would be stoked to learn all Sky knew, and when he was enrolled at Alfea, he'd be assigned a roommate. How handy was that? The school officially arranged a friend for you.

Sky had been certain having a roommate would be great.

Sky had to admit Riven wasn't what he'd had in mind, but he and Riven had known each other a while and were pretty friendly at archery tournaments. They'd had several pleasant-enough conversations about arrowheads. Plus, Riven did have potential on the field. If he'd listen to Sky and shape up, he'd actually be good. And Riven was funny sometimes, though a lot of what he said was disrespectful, so Sky didn't encourage him by smiling at it. Sky had been hoping for a fellow soldier, dedicated to duty like he was, so they could have a brothers-in-arms bond like his dad and Silva had. An unbreakable bond, stronger than death.

There was nobody at Alfea who Sky felt was remotely a candidate to have an unbreakable bond with. So Riven was pretty much Sky's best friend, and Sky would continue helping him out during lessons.

As long as Silva permitted it. Sky would never cross his commander.

Sky gave Silva a grateful smile. "I can keep my skill levels up by myself. Hey, I run ten circuits around the grounds every day, sunrise and sunset. Just like you and Dad used to."

He thought Silva might be pleased by that.

Silva did smile faintly, but it didn't last. "When I say I want you to be like your father . . . you know I mean that I want you to be better, right?"

How am I supposed to do that? Sky's inner insubordinate voice, which sounded more and more like Riven these days,

31

asked. *There are no monsters left to fight! How am I supposed to outdo a war hero when there's no more war?*

"I'll try," Sky said.

Whenever he felt like Silva's expectations of him were unreasonable, Sky knew he was letting everybody down. Silva just wanted Sky to be the best he could be. It was how Silva showed he cared about Sky. Every time Sky was the best, Sky proved he was worth caring for.

He'd run twelve circuits around the grounds from now on, he promised himself, giving Silva a smile and setting off. It wasn't being a war hero, but it was something.

From this distance and this direction, the branches of the trees cut shadows across the gleaming blue of the Barrier, their protection against evil, as though someone had torn pieces in it. Nobody had, Sky knew. Alfea was safe. Thanks to the sacrifices of heroes like his dad.

Can't I call you Dad? Sky had asked Silva once, when he was little and stupid, leaning against Silva's legs on a day when he'd done especially well at training, so he thought Silva might be more likely to agree. Silva had taken Sky by the shoulders and shook him, roughly enough so tears sprang into Sky's eyes. Sky didn't let the tears fall.

"No," Silva said with cold fury. "You had a father, Sky. He was a hero. He saved lives. Neither of us can ever forget him."

Silva's eyes bored through Sky sometimes, looking at Sky so hard it felt like Silva was looking through him at someone else. People said Sky looked a lot like his dad.

Sky understood that day. Silva was raising him because of his dad. It was betraying his dad and Silva both, to want a dad who was here to hug him.

Racing someone only he could see under the long shadows of the trees at Alfea, Sky pushed himself further, and felt his lungs burn.

LIGHT

Stella stood in the courtyard, with the setting sun and an artful daub of magic mood-lighting framing her curled golden hair. She was wearing a shimmering lavender blouse and a long white leather skirt. Ricki had helped her choose subtle amethyst art deco earrings to complete the outfit. She looked like a fashionable dream of spring.

And her boyfriend was late. Stella tapped the stacked heel of her ivory boot against the cobblestones as she watched Sky dash into the courtyard and run up to give her a hug.

"Ew!" protested Stella, putting her palm flat against his chest and pushing him back. "Sweaty—sweatier than usual! Why?"

"Silva suggested I run some extra laps and I kinda lost track of time," Sky explained. As Stella glared at him accusingly, he added hastily, "I'm sorry."

Stella waited, and then felt forced to feed him his next line. Honestly, men were hopeless.

"What do you think of my outfit?"

"You look great," Sky told her.

Such truth! Stella beamed at him.

He leaned in, kissed her cheek, and spoiled the compliment by adding, "You always look great, Stel."

Did he not understand saying that meant her special effort had gone for nothing?

"That's sweet, if totally insufficient. Look all you want, just don't touch the hair," said Stella, and patted Sky's shoulder forgivingly as she pushed him away. She wanted him in a good mood so he'd be amenable to carrying out her plans. "Babe, I was thinking. I always have so much fun on our dates."

"Oh." Sky blinked at her. "Good."

"But I was thinking we might try something a little different," she continued.

Sky brightened. "Yeah?" He must have thought it was a wonderful idea, as well he should.

"Wouldn't it be super fun to have a triple date?" Stella asked. When Sky just stared at her, she spread her hands so her family ring caught the dying light and sparkled brilliantly. "Like a double date, but even more fun. Me and you, and Ilaria and her guy, Matt, and—"

Sky's frown came naturally, like a judgmental flinch. Usually, Sky was pleasant to everyone, which Stella appreciated, but when he disapproved, he was seldom able to hide it.

Stella's voice came out sharper than intended. "What's your objection to Ilaria and Matt?"

"... The dude's kind of disrespectful to women," Sky mumbled, almost under his breath. "When it's just us guys."

"Yes?" asked Stella. "Well, as a woman, I think I should be the judge of that. Care to repeat some of what he's said?"

As expected, Sky opened and closed his mouth, clearly incapable of saying anything disrespectful. Sky was a true gentleman. It really held him back.

"Glad that's settled," said Stella. "Then I think we should set up someone with Ricki."

Sky's strained expression smoothed out into a smile of genuine pleasure. "Good idea. Ricki's great."

Stella knew Ricki was great; that was why she was doing all this. Once Ricki formed a power couple, Ricki would be an acceptable roommate for Stella.

She waited for Sky to catch up. "Do you have any suggestions for Ricki's date?"

There was a pause.

"What do you think of Riven?" Sky asked carefully.

Stella blinked. "I never think of Riven."

She was barely aware of Riven, Sky's vaguely weaselly roommate, who thought his leather jacket made him look cooler than it did. Sky had taken a fancy to him, but Sky had once bottle-fed five kittens at the palace when the mother cat died. Sky was drawn to pathetic, needy creatures.

And you, a voice in Stella's mind said, but Stella banished that like the princess she was.

"If not Riven," Sky asked, "then who? Sam?"

"What's Sam?" Stella asked. "Wait, isn't he an Earth Fairy? Sky, please! I can't stand Earth Fairies. Earth Fairies mean nature, and nature is dirty. Don't you know any second years?"

Sky shrugged helplessly. Sky was a bit of a loner, dedicated to doing his duty and building his muscle tone. Stella appreciated the lean muscles and everything, but networking skills would be even better.

Alfea was a wonderful school, but there was definitely room for improvement when it came to the heating and the eye candy. Stella's mind ran through the options available. There weren't many.

Reluctantly, she reconsidered Sky's roommate.

Riven had a habit of eyeing Stella as though he was making sarcastic remarks about her in his head, which was some nerve coming from someone as pretentiously scruffy as Riven. She had long dismissed Riven as a person. Now, however, she considered him as an accessory for Ricki.

She supposed he wasn't actually bad-looking. He should wash more, but that was the case with almost all boys, Stella was saddened to admit. Riven definitely had a mean streak, and Ricki could stand to get meaner. She was almost as nice as Sky, though at least Ricki would gossip with Stella. Maybe Ricki and Riven could make it work. Stella had read in *Fabulous Fairy* that couples should learn from each other.

Fine, it was settled. Riven would teach Ricki how to be unpleasant, and Ricki could teach Riven how to dress, speak, and socially interact with others.

Stella gave Sky a smile, granting royal permission.

"All right," she announced. "Tell your annoying roommate that it's his lucky day."

EARTH

The sun was sinking through the high windows of the greenhouse, and Terra was almost ready to give up, when the door slammed open and the person she'd been waiting for finally stumbled in.

Terra sprang up with joy that swiftly turned to horror. "Riven, you're soaking wet! What happened?"

Riven took down the hood of his hoodie. When he was sneaking to the greenhouse after hours, he always put his hood up, as if he truly believed this made him more difficult to spot. His hair was wet, too. Another black eye was forming.

"Got dumped in the lake," Riven reported shortly.

"Sky is a monster!" Terra exclaimed, appalled.

Riven shook his head. His hair had gone all flat and sad from the water, and droplets flew across the lab table. "Wasn't Sky. This time it was Mikey."

"Oh no, not Mikey!" Terra fretted. "Mikey is huge!"

"Noticed that myself," said Riven.

He spoke in his usual sardonic tones, but he wasn't flipping his knife around like usual—poor Riven, he thought knife flipping made him look badass—and he was shivering inside his leather jacket. Terra made a swift decision. Something Must Be Done.

"You need a warm blanket," she declared. "I'll get the one my grandma Dahlia knitted. Also I will make you a soothing herbal tea. I mixed it myself. It's super soothing!"

"Nah," said Riven. Terra was about to sternly inform him that he'd do as he was told, but then Riven added, "Let's get the crate open. It's almost sunset."

Terra was diverted by this undeniable truth. "Oh, okay! I already took out the nails, so all we have to do is lever up the top. I waited for you."

"Thanks." Riven glanced her way and gave her a smile that lasted about half a second. She really had to pay attention in order to catch his smiles. They were terribly rare.

At the start of school this year, Sam had given her the cold shoulder, and Terra had slunk off to the greenhouse to brood and prune. She figured she might as well make herself useful while she was miserable.

Except she found someone else being miserable in the greenhouse ahead of her. He was sitting under the spreading leaves of a huge fern, and he was crying.

Terra approached cautiously. "Boy," she said, "why are you crying?"

When he looked up, Terra saw why. Riven had two black eyes. Later, she discovered he also had a sprained ankle.

She was grateful for the sprained ankle. The sprain stopped Riven from making an effective getaway as he tried to run from his humiliation and Terra tried to persuade him not to. She explained who she was, that she didn't even go to Alfea, and she didn't matter at all. Even if she wanted to gossip about Riven crying in the greenhouse, she had nobody to tell. Terra had never been so grateful for her own ability to talk a mile a minute.

After Riven stopped attempting to escape, Terra fetched him ointments and unguents she'd crafted herself. She made Riven's two black eyes go away in three days. After that, once the school day was over, Riven would come slinking into the greenhouse like an alley cat too proud to admit it wanted to be fed. He was lonely, Terra believed. Boy, did Terra get that.

She taught Riven how to make all the ointments and unguents she knew, and then told him about the healing properties of certain plants. He got pretty into it. Even though he tried to pretend he wasn't interested, Terra could tell.

Now when there was a delivery of an especially cool plant, Terra would wait to unbox it with Riven. This was the most awesome delivery yet.

She didn't want to make a big deal out of waiting, though, so she said carelessly, "I kept myself amused with other things. Do you know I followed Headmistress Dowling today? She was sneaking off through the woods to a secret location. I mean, I assume it was a secret location. She was going through a magic door, so it probably wasn't a short-cut to a bathroom."

"Was she?" Riven blinked. "I saw her assistant creeping off through the woods, too. Hey, think he's hitting that?"

"*Riven!*" Terra yelped, and Riven winced.

She was sorry about his poor head, which must hurt from being punched in the face, but that was no reason for bad behavior. Riven had an unfortunately filthy mind, but Terra firmly believed he could learn better. He was clever, even if he acted so stupid.

"Do you think that's an appropriate way to talk about our headmistress?"

"No . . ." mumbled Riven.

"Let's leave aside the long history of disrespect for strong women authority figures," said Terra.

"Yes . . . let's . . ." muttered Riven.

"Have you considered that gossip is poison for a working environment?" Terra asked severely. "I should know! I can make thirty-four poisons myself. Five are untraceable."

Riven grimaced. "I don't think I want that soothing tea, after all."

"Of course, now we're discussing literal poisons, while

before I meant the metaphorical poison that can be dripped in people's ears, particularly in reference to women, particularly in reference to their romantic lives and sexual pasts—"

"Wow, I know!" exclaimed Riven. "I know, okay? Can we open the crate before the sun sets!"

Terra relented. Riven was injured, after all. She skipped over to the crate, which was resting between a smooth sandstone wall and a black lab desk, and shoved the lid off.

"Behold the truthbells," declared Terra.

Within the crate was a planter, dark earth crowded with flowers. The truthbells were shaped like bluebells. Instead of blue, the flowers were a pearly gray that might have looked dull any other time. Not now. As the dying light of the sun caught the petals, each bell shone with silvery radiance.

"So cool," Riven said under his breath.

Terra, who entirely agreed, grinned hugely to herself.

"If you distill both petals and pollen into a potion at exactly the right time, it becomes a truth potion. That's why it had to be sent to my dad," she said, bragging a little. "In the hands of anyone less skilled, who doesn't time the collection of the pollen right or get the volumes of the potion precisely correct, it would become a deadly poison."

"Badass" was Riven's approving verdict.

Riven's head must have been hurting a lot, because he let his guard down enough to lean his head against Terra's shoulder. Terra made a sympathetically distressed sound and patted him on the back. Riven really must have been feeling lousy. He even rubbed his cheek against the wool of her sweater, just a little.

"Oh, Riven," said Terra. "What happened to you?"

"I hate it here, Ter," Riven mumbled.

"I know," Terra murmured comfortingly.

She looked out of the flowing tracery of the greenhouse windows onto the grounds of Alfea. This was her home, and Terra had always found it beautiful. They said light was different in the fairy realms, less blazing bright yellow than in the First World, especially when fey twilight drew in before the long dew-dropping hours of night. In the fairy realms, all light intertwined with shadow. All light was tinged gray and green, traveling in shafts through leaves in a dewy wood. In Terra's home, light rippled with a fairy wind, and the gently moving landscape of the earth was like a living sea. Land under wave.

But if you were drowning, you couldn't see beauty.

Clearly, Riven was being horribly bullied, but he was too embarrassed to talk about it. Terra was shocked by Sky's wanton cruelty.

All Terra really wanted was someone who needed her and wouldn't leave her. Next year, Terra would have lots of friends, but right now Riven was her only friend, and it was her job to look after him.

This could not go on. She was certain Riven would like

it more at Alfea if people stopped bullying him. So, Terra decided, they were going to stop. Terra would see to that.

Plans were most efficient when deadlines were set. Terra intended to be very busy during orientation, collecting her future new friends.

That gave her three days. By the time Orientation Day came around, Terra would make sure Riven was safe.

WATER

It was three days until Orientation Day, until Aisha finally got to see Alfea, and Aisha was getting ready to swim. Aisha swam every day. No excuses. If you let yourself skip one day, you'd skip others. Breaking one rule meant you were willing to break them all. That led to loss of discipline. And loss of discipline led to the worst thing Aisha could think of: letting down her team. Aisha would never do that. Aisha's team had won awards. Aisha was the pride and joy of every swim coach she'd ever had.

Magic wasn't swimming.

She sat on the side of the outdoor swimming pool and tried to summon dewdrops from the grass to form a curtain in the air. The dewdrops rose, but then her control slipped and dewdrops hit her face like a hundred spitting cats. Aisha spluttered, shutting her eyes.

She loved the water. She'd always moved through the element easier than she did in the air. She wore floaty dresses when she wasn't in athletic gear, to remind herself of floating in the water. Most of her statement earrings had blue stones: blue topaz and turquoise and sapphire. She'd often thought about streaking her dreads with cobalt blue to recall the sea an hour before sunset, her favorite shade of blue. She'd always been able to excel when she pushed herself. Aisha was a Water Fairy, so she should be able to summon and control the water as she chose.

Yet somehow, her power kept slipping through her fingers.

And this week she was going to Alfea's Orientation Day, to the school she wanted to attend so badly. They didn't accept you if your magic wasn't powerful enough. But hers was. It *was*! It must be. She had responsibilities.

Aisha summoned the dewdrops again, trying to catch them in a tiny pool in the hollow of her hands. This time the dew sprayed out wildly between her fingers like a fountain gone rogue.

What if a teacher or a mentor at the Orientation Day asked to see her magic? What if Aisha embarrassed herself, and people thought she'd be a liability to any team she was on?

For the first time in years, Aisha was tempted to skip her daily swim and focus on her magic. But she knew that was weakness. If she doubted herself, she'd choke.

She slid into the swimming pool. As soon as the water closed over her head, Aisha felt herself become calm. She propelled her body down the lane, arms falling into their accustomed rhythm. The markers kept her focused and moving swift and sure. Her destination was clear, and her plan formed.

Orientation Day was coming. Aisha would finally see Alfea, the famous school where she would learn to use her magic. Aisha was sure once she was taught, she could apply herself to her lessons. She'd focus with all the discipline she'd learned over her years of training. Sometimes she'd stall out when training, but she'd always overcome that and she would do the same now. She'd win out, just the way she had at sports. What she needed to find at Alfea was a mentor. Something like a magic coach, who would guide her.

Aisha had always been able to accomplish everything she set her mind to. It wasn't luck. It was sheer hard work that had earned the respect and admiration of every team and every team leader she'd ever had. One day, she'd be a leader herself. She needed to learn more first.

When Orientation Day happened, Aisha knew she would see the path ahead of her, clear as a channel of water. She would find a leader she could follow, and people who would be her new teammates.

For now, she just had to keep swimming.

DO MOST BITTER WRONG

Dear Sir,

It is as you suspected. Dowling has come across a message that may indicate a key part of Rosalind's last scheme.

I don't know precisely what Rosalind's secret is. Dowling has not permitted me close enough to see what was written, but I recognized Rosalind's writing itself, and I seized every opportunity to read Dowling's notes researching the object's location.

I have been using the listening device you so helpfully enchanted for me night and day, but so far she has confided in nobody. She left the school grounds during work hours and without an appointment today. She has not done such a thing in all the years I have been working for her. Naturally, I followed her, and I can confirm she moved through a bespelled doorway into another world. Consulting the tracking stones, I determined her destination was the First World.

Fairies do not often tend to wander into that dull world full of weeping. Not until now. Not unless there is something to be gained from going.

I will not let a move or a sign from her escape me.

Rest assured, whatever Dowling has found will be ours.

Yours respectfully,

Callum Hunter

Fairy Tale #2

My heart would brim with dreams about the times
When we bent down above the fading coals
And talked of the dark folk who live in souls.

—W. B. Yeats

SPECIALIST

Stella had given Sky a mission, and he'd accepted it. Now he had to accomplish it. Somehow.

Already the mission wasn't going as smoothly as he'd hoped.

"So, you're back late," Sky said as Riven sunk into their room, long after Sky had returned from his and Stella's date.

Sky and Riven's teal-painted room was nice, with a desk in between their beds and a window, a dartboard, and even a low sofa. Riven had introduced the dartboard, and seemed pleased when Sky said it was cool. Riven had deflated when Sky added that now they could work on perfecting their aim. Sky didn't get why that was wrong. Precise aim was cool.

Sky had taken the bed that was pushed up in the corner, farther away from the window. It didn't bother him, and he'd hoped his new roommate would be pleased to have the other bed.

That was before he learned his roommate was never pleased with anything.

Riven tossed his pretentious leather jacket at a chair rather than hanging it up, because coat hooks were apparently for conformists. Then he took his knife out of his pocket and started tossing it around, which Riven believed looked cool. Riven was mistaken. He'd spent the first few months of school with small cuts all over his hands. Sky was worried he was going to lose fingers.

"Were you waiting up, honey?"

"Where do you go after class?" Sky hesitated. "Do you have a secret girlfriend?"

Riven's whole body tensed up. Sky had never actually asked where Riven ran off to after class. Mostly because Sky figured Riven was going to sulk among the trees. Riven loved sulking and also trees. That would be embarrassing for Riven to admit, and for Sky to hear.

"No." Riven's voice was strained. "I don't have a secret girlfriend."

Cool. Already one worry out of the way. This mission was going great.

"Are you interested in dating someone?"

"I know all the fairies think you're the swooniest Specialist, but do-gooders aren't my thing."

Sky rolled his eyes and shoved Riven, then remembered Riven was still holding a knife and looked hastily at his hands. Thankfully, Riven retained his grip on the knife plus all his fingers.

"Not interested in someone who has such lousy form when it comes to knifework, dude," said Sky, teasing but also very serious. The knifework was terrible.

"Stella slices and dices pretty well?" Riven raised an eyebrow. "Yeah, that tracks. The princess is terrifying and you're gonna get beheaded."

"Stel's great, actually."

"Sounds fake, but okay!" said Riven.

Sky's roommate seemed in a worse mood than usual, and he wasn't a little ray of sunshine at the best of times.

Sky bit his lip. "Is this about you getting beat up by Mikey?"

"Why must we discuss me getting beat up by Mikey with everyone watching?"

Sky stared. "Everyone was watching because we were in class. That's how you learn. And you could beat Mikey, if only you—"

"Believed in myself?" Riven scoffed.

"I was gonna say used an efficient choke hold," said Sky. "But you can do the believing-in-yourself thing, too, I guess."

Riven's technique was a lot better than Mikey's. Sky had seen to that.

Riven sighed. "Is this going somewhere, or are we just having one of our awkward roommate convos?"

That was another reason that Sky's mission was a good idea. Riven and Sky spent a lot of time together, in class and also training after hours, which Sky made Riven do. It was cool to have a regular sparring partner.

Still, it seemed like a best-friend thing to socialize other than sparring. Sky didn't want to spend time brooding among the trees. He had no feelings about trees. This would get Riven out of the trees.

"What do you think of Ricki?"

Riven seemed startled. "Ricki's fun."

"Right?" Sky was relieved they agreed. It didn't happen much. "She's great."

Ricki was Sky's favorite of Stella's friends. If you asked Sky, and Stella never did, the others only cared that Stella was a princess and wouldn't have Stella's back if she was in trouble. He thought Ricki might. And Ricki always made time to talk to Sky and get to know him, which was really nice of her.

"Are you dumping Stella and getting with Ricki?" asked Riven. "Good call. Great call, and thanks for telling me first, because now I can move all my stuff out of our room before Stella sets everything on fire."

Sky stared in disbelief. "I would never dump Stella. Why would I dump Stella?"

Riven opened his mouth with the air of a man who had much to say.

"Remember how you and I and Stella and Ricki hung out at the Senior Specialists' party?" Sky said hurriedly.

Sky had got a little silly and done his impression of Silva. When he was a kid, he'd talked with Silva's accent, but it made Silva upset because he thought it meant Sky was growing up rough. So Sky didn't talk that way anymore, but he could. Ricki and Riven both seemed to think the impression was hilarious.

Later, Sky worried his impression was disrespectful, and he didn't want to do it again unless he trusted the people he was with to take it the right way. But he'd had fun at the time. It felt as if they were all friends that night.

"That was actually a blast," admitted Riven.

"Until you had too much to drink," Sky felt obliged to point out.

"Wow, sorry I know how to have a good time at a party."

"You vomited in five places," said Sky.

He'd had to practically carry Riven back to their room while Riven cried and, weirdly, begged for herbal tea.

"Live fast, die young, bad girls do it well," Riven informed him.

Sky suppressed a grin and gave Riven the look of total judgment he felt Riven deserved. "What would you say to a triple date? Me and Stella, Matt and Ilaria, you and Ricki."

Riven was staring. "You want *me* to date *Ricki?*"

"Uh," said Sky. "You did say she was fun. And you don't say positive things about girls, so—"

"I say many positive things about many girls! Your praying mantis of a girlfriend is an outlier and shouldn't be counted!"

"You don't know her," said Sky. "She's a great girl. She's gonna be a great queen one day."

Riven's eyebrows went airborne. "Stella? She cares more about good lighting than good works."

Like Riven cared about good works. "Do you wanna go out on a triple date or not?"

"Do you not get why this is hilarious?"

Sky didn't, but he didn't want to admit it. Riven was funny

and Sky got a kick out of his jokes. They were jokes Sky never would've let himself make. But when the jokes got cruel, Sky wanted nothing to do with them. There was an odd gleam in Riven's eyes, which made Sky think now was one of those times.

"Forget about this being hilarious," Sky said, instead of admitting uncertainty. Silva would never do that. "Yes or no?"

"Yeah, sure, why not?" said Riven, and laughed.

There were times when Sky didn't like Riven that much. To illustrate his amusement, Riven started tossing his knife up into the air and catching it. He almost dropped it once and almost cut himself twice.

Sky'd had enough. He confiscated the knife from Riven and demonstrated. "Watch, this is how you hold it."

"Quit looking down on me," said Riven, and went to bed.

Sky looked at the lump under the covers that was Riven, sighed, and figured the date was on. He tossed and caught the knife neatly, watching the blade spin and catch the moonlight in midair.

Mission accomplished.

LIGHT

"Welcome to the first meeting for the Committee for Organizing Orientation Day," said Stella. "COD for short! I cut out the extra *O* as obsolete."

She gazed around the table in the courtyard with a beatific smile.

"Oh no, this is a trap," Riven muttered.

Riven looked even more weaselly close up and in direct sunlight. Sky was such a kind, generous person, so Stella was puzzled. Why had Sky not taken pity on Riven and told him that skipping shaving was a bad idea?

Maybe Sky didn't know. Sky was thankfully clean-shaven, but Stella had dark thoughts about Silva's facial-hair situation. He had stubble that she worried at any moment might turn horribly toward a goatee. Silva was handsome otherwise in a stern-father, aged way, and Sky believed Headmaster Silva could do no wrong, but Stella considered a goatee unforgivable.

As royalty should, Stella decided to be merciful. "Here's a tip, Riven. The artful stubble? It doesn't make you look badass. It makes you look as if you can't shave right."

Riven made a face at Stella. Some people didn't appreciate benevolence.

They sat around a round stone table in the courtyard, under a casement window and a streamer of ivy. Matt and Ilaria were making out wildly, chairs pushed together, as they often did. Riven, Sky, Stella, and Ricki were assembled at different points around the table, staring at one another. Riven kept sliding glances over at Matt and Ilaria's make-out session, that pervert. Stella had placed a flicker of magic light in one of the stained-glass windowpanes, pouring a gentle shower of aquamarine-tinted radiance over her artful braid and her smart blazer.

As soon as Ricki had sat down, she'd clocked the light, said, "Gorgeous girl," and given Stella a hug and a wink.

This would all be worth it, for Ricki.

Stella had worked out a scheme. Ricki was beautiful and had so much going for her. She wouldn't just give up on life and agree to date Riven right away. Ricki had to be eased into it by seeing how much fun group dates could be, under the cunning guise of a committee. Then she'd come around. One-on-one dates were a little boring; everybody knew that.

Plus, Stella's mother said public appearances and charity work were the most important part of the job for royalty. This Orientation Day was Stella's natural habitat.

"Ms. Dowling was unavailable, so I checked in with Headmaster Silva," Stella informed them all. "I said that we were delighted to volunteer to help with the final preparations for the day. Can you believe it, Silva said they didn't have a plan for lighting?"

Ricki laughed. "Lucky them, Stella's on the case."

"Hey, I think I might be a secret fairy with a powerful magic heritage," declared Riven. "I think I feel my wings coming in, like in the old stories. Oh no, wait, that's my ears trying to detach from my head and fly away. Are you unfamiliar with the concept of volunteering? Do you think it means 'being commanded by royalty'? Princess, that's not what it means."

Stella was outraged to see Sky's mouth do the thing that meant he wanted to smile. Even though Sky didn't smile, it was still a betrayal. Stella had no idea why Sky found Riven amusing. It occurred to her that Sky might have bad taste in people, but that made no sense. Sky was dating her, so he obviously had the best taste in people ever.

"I haven't issued any commands," Stella informed Riven haughtily. Though she could! "Naturally, I told my best girls about my committee plans."

Ricki had cheerfully agreed, game for anything, and Ilaria had shrugged and said, *Sure, why not?*

"Did she tell you?" Riven consulted with Sky, inclining his poseur-messy, light-brown head toward Sky's perfect golden one.

Sky had such good hair, and he wore fantastic cropped jackets. If Riven infected her boyfriend with bad style, Stella would slay him.

"Uh, no, she didn't," said Sky.

Stella glared at him.

"Off with his head," muttered Riven, and this time Sky did crack a smile.

"Sky!" exclaimed Stella, shocked by this base treachery, and Sky stopped smiling.

"Ah, romance," murmured Riven. "Or as others call it, indentured servitude."

Sky gave him a reproving look. "Come on, Riv."

"Yes, come on," Ricki chimed in, sending Sky a warm

smile, then transferring it to Riven, whereupon the smile became understandably cooler. "We'll have fun, won't we?"

Riven, it seemed, wasn't immune to Ricki's easy charm. "Well . . ."

Stella and Sky exchanged a covert glance of victory.

"Just like we did at the Senior Specialists' party, before you got sloppy drunk."

Ricki's grin was mischievous. After a moment, Riven grinned grudgingly back. "That was a good time."

The Senior Specialists' party was traditionally one of the most scandalous occasions of the year. Stella had found the perfect outfit and arrived in the abandoned East Wing on Sky's arm, but the party was all downhill after her grand entrance. The whole business had struck Stella as undignified. She'd been more out of control than she liked, and everyone else had been even further out of her control.

Ricki had seemed in her element at the Senior Specialists' party, dashing around giggling, getting Riven and Sky to make snow fairies in the fallen leaves. She'd hooked an arm around Riven's and Sky's necks and coaxed them into singing with her, Ricki's own head tipped back, totally unself-conscious.

Stella didn't know how to be anything but self-conscious. If anyone ever saw her in an unguarded moment . . . she didn't know what they would see. She shivered. She didn't even want to know.

"You okay, Stel?" asked Sky, sounding concerned, and for a wild moment Stella thought he'd read her mind and they were soul mates.

Instead he shrugged off his cropped jacket and offered it to her. It was spring, but there was still a touch of cold in the air, like a lonely ghost had reached out for Stella. She shook her head reprovingly at Sky, who should have known better than to think she'd spoil her outfit, but when he put his arm around her, she leaned into his warm support gratefully. He shored her up, keeping her safe and staying beside her so she wasn't alone. As he had done ever since they were kids.

"Just find your warm inner place," Riven said, mocking.

"You find your warm inner place," Stella shot back. "Me, I'll grab a blanket or my boyfriend. Don't you wish you had someone to keep you warm?"

Riven glared, and Stella preened. She was such a consummate multitasker, scoring off Riven and also letting Ricki know Riven was single. Like all Stella's plans, this was going so great.

"I'm in hell," Riven muttered.

So great!

"I'm on lighting," Stella continued, confidence recharging the longer Sky kept his arm around her. "Ricki and Ilaria are designing posters."

"Would you help hang up the posters, Sky?" Ricki asked shyly. "Since you're tall."

"Oh, sure." Sky was always obliging. "Riv?"

Riven, who was never obliging, grunted.

"You're not tall," Stella observed. "Or handsome. Or polite. But surely you can hang posters."

Matt and Ilaria surfaced, with a smacking of lips and Ilaria's hair disarranged. Stella was privately horrified. She and Sky didn't make a show of themselves in public like this.

"Are we still talking about the committee?" Ilaria asked with a scarlet-lipped yawn. "Does nobody have any good gossip?"

That was not in the spirit of the committee! Stella frowned.

Riven leaned forward, eager suddenly. "I think Ms. Dowling is having a secret affair with her secretary."

"What!" Stella jumped right out of Sky's protective arms. "Why are you like this? Ms. Dowling wouldn't do that! You have a nasty mind."

People respected Ms. Dowling. They looked up to her. She was the steady center of Alfea. She wouldn't take advantage of an employee.

But then, Stella couldn't forget her mother. Stella knew better than anyone that people were never entirely what they seemed.

Ilaria was rubbing her hands together in glee. "Explain your interesting theory, Riven, wasn't it?"

Riven grinned at her. "Uh . . . I saw Ms. Dowling

sneaking off into the grounds, then she passed through an enchanted door. And minutes later, I saw Callum creeping, too. Heading in the same direction she was. Why would he be following her around if he didn't have the hots for her?"

She'd been right. Riven was a total perv. "Maybe he wanted to inform her of something, in a secretarial capacity!" Stella snapped.

"Callum stood behind a tree when he saw me," said Riven. "Why would he hide if he was blamelessly secretary-ing about?"

"You know, that's pretty convincing," admitted Matt.

Ilaria's eyes sparkled. "And juicy!"

Riven looked smug. Stella didn't have to put up with this. She drew herself up with icy royal hauteur and said, "It's perfectly obvious to anyone that there is a sensible explanation."

Matt made a rude noise. "Like what?"

Stella was starting to see why Sky disliked Matt. He was kind of a meathead, but many Specialists were.

"I don't know the explanation yet," she admitted, "but if I cared to, I could find out right away."

"Wanna bet, Princess?" Riven sneered.

She'd had it with this guy. Stella leaned back in her seat, folded her arms, and lifted her chin so the light magic struck the gold in her braid. "I'd love to, peasant. As we go about our business as the Committee for Organizing Orientation Day, I have no doubt that we will have many opportunities to observe Callum. And Ms. Dowling, once we find out where she's run off to."

Even though Ms. Dowling had only been gone a day, Stella felt uneasy about her absence. She was usually *here*, anchoring the whole castle. It was oddly nice to have an adult you felt you could rely on. If Stella was ever in trouble, sometimes she thought she might go to Ms. Dowling.

Not that Stella was ever likely to be in trouble. Stella's life was pretty much perfect.

"Maybe she's run off to her secret love nest with Callum," Ilaria joked.

She almost tipped over sideways to nudge Riven. Stella hadn't set this up so that Ilaria could get along with Riven. Ilaria already had a boyfriend. She was already part of a power couple! Ricki was the one who required a boyfriend, though the more time Stella spent with Riven, the more unsure she became about his suitability.

Sky had taken Riven under his wing, and he'd assured Stella he was training Riven, so she'd assumed he was teaching Riven basic social graces. Stella was starting to have the awful suspicion that Sky was just talking about fighting. As though hitting people with big sticks was more than a tiny part of being powerful.

As with most matters, it would be best if Stella

personally assumed command. "When I win our bet," said Stella, "everyone can stop making those terrible jokes. And you, Riven? You should do whatever I ask you. For a week."

She would issue instructions on how Riven should dress and behave, and Ricki would be charmed by the new, improved version. Riven would be grateful, too. It would also be nice for Sky; Riven was an embarrassment to be seen with at present.

Basically, Stella spread light wherever she went. Metaphorically as well as literally. She glowed with satisfaction.

"What about me?" demanded Riven.

He was so uncouth.

Stella felt her mouth tighten. "What about you?"

"What do I get if I win?" asked Riven. "Will *you* do whatever *I* want?"

Stella sniffed. "Don't be absurd."

"How about this?" said Riven. "No using light magic. For a week."

Ugh, what a pest. His eyes were a horrible cold green-gray color, watching her as if he had any idea what it would mean to live her life alone in the shadows. As if he saw her clearly and didn't think much of her. How dare he! She was a princess! As if she cared what that loser Riven thought.

Sky and Ricki were watching, too. She wished Sky still had his arm around her, but Stella was the one who'd moved away from him, and now she was too embarrassed to crawl back. She held her head high, as her mother commanded that a princess must.

"Fine," she answered carelessly. "But you needn't think you can spin this out. You'll have to prove your little theory fast."

Riven shrugged, and claimed rashly, "I can prove it in a couple days."

"Marvelous." Stella gave him a glittering smile. "Prove it by Orientation Day, or prepare to be my Specialist servant."

The committee meeting broke up soon after that. Stella stayed behind to design her lighting plan for Orientation Day.

Against her considerable will, Stella found her mind returning to the Senior Specialists' party. Ricki and Sky had got on so well that night.

In a sickeningly vivid flash of memory, Stella recalled Ricki's arm around Sky's neck, their voices echoing off the walls of the East Wing, both of them singing about freedom. The light magic she'd set in the stained-glass window flashed too bright, enough to send lancing pain through Stella's head before she swiftly extinguished it.

Stella didn't like not being at the center of things, where she belonged. She hadn't enjoyed that party. But she was taking charge, and she was certain she would adore Orientation Day.

SPECIALIST

Sometimes Sky was hilarious. Never on purpose, of course. This triple date was the worst idea anyone had ever had, and not just because Riven had been lured into a bet and agreed to decorate the whole school.

But at least he'd finally met some cool people.

He'd never really talked to Ilaria before. She was one of Stella's posse, and Riven steered clear of the ladies-in-waiting. Except for Ricki, who'd pulled him out of a corner and got him to dance at the Senior Specialists' party. He liked Ricki.

He wasn't gonna start dating Ricki, though, because Ricki was clearly hung up on Sky.

He couldn't believe Stella had missed it. Stella was so highly strung, she made nervous thoroughbred horses look like happy tortoises. Her deranged eyes reflected both her eerily constant magic mood lighting and her inner lunatic fires . . . but she didn't strike Riven as a dummy.

If Stella didn't know, she didn't want to know.

"It must be so much fun to be roommates with Sky," said Ricki.

She was leading Riven, Ilaria, and Matt around the castle, showing them what she believed would be ideal spots for posters. Only Ricki seemed terribly interested in poster placement.

"Every day a thrill," said Riven. "For him."

Ricki laughed. Laughter came easy to her. Riven didn't understand why Sky would choose someone like Stella, bright and cold and about as much fun as a glacier, over someone like Ricki.

Maybe Sky wouldn't, in the end. Wouldn't that stun the princess?

"I wouldn't mind seeing Sky come out of the shower every day," drawled Ilaria.

"Yes, it's great," said Riven. In the startled pause that followed, he added, "I'm thinking of selling his photos to *Solaria Weekly*. 'The Princess's Man . . . Uncovered!'"

Ilaria snickered. "People are always stopping and asking for a picture with Stella. Is it the same with Sky? Our little celebrities."

"They're the perfect couple," murmured Ricki.

She sounded slightly sad, which was unusual for Ricki. Maybe she was mournfully thinking that she had no chance with Sky. Maybe she was actually in love with Stella.

Riven didn't know. All he knew was that Ricki didn't like *him* that way. What a surprise.

Out of the corner of his eye, he saw Matt pretend to puke, and he grinned and fell back a step so he was walking with Matt and Ilaria instead of Ricki. When Matt and Riven headed back for the Specialists' Hall, its high gray walls like a prison and its iron curlicues and spikes a chain around the glass dome, Ilaria came, too.

They seemed to really like each other. They were very handsy.

Riven occupied himself by tossing his knife from hand to hand, a move he'd picked up when he updated his look from . . . the way it had been before. He was getting the hang of the knife toss. He slightly fumbled once, but Matt and Ilaria didn't see. It was lucky they were otherwise occupied.

"Nice to get to know you, man," said Matt when they paused their making out for Ilaria to redo her lipstick. "You and Sky are always training together. Nobody else gets a look in. You're pretty good, aren't you? Saw you sparring with Mikey."

"Yeah, I'm sure that was memorable," said Riven. "Nobody else gets pulverized with my special flair."

"No, man, you were good until you flinched," said Matt. "You've got to remember: no mercy. Maybe you can't take Sky down—who can?—but I'd say you have a good chance against anyone else in your year. Even a beast like Mikey."

Sky had said something like that, but that was insufferable Sky pitying him. Matt sounded as if he really meant it. Riven thought back to Sky suggesting a choke hold. Maybe Riven could've tried harder, rather than privately admitting defeat at the start of the fight. He'd gotten used to retreat.

". . . Thanks," muttered Riven, hoping that didn't sound too weak and sincere.

Matt shrugged. "No problem. You're a better man than me. I couldn't stand training with Sky every day. He and Stella seem nice and all, but . . . very uptight."

His tone spoke volumes.

"Yeah," said Riven, trying to sound relaxed and casual. They were both chill. A cool couple of guys, hanging out.

"Hate a high-maintenance chick," Matt continued, in a lower voice so Ilaria wouldn't hear.

"I guess," said Riven.

Matt flashed Riven a just-kidding, guys-being-guys grin, and Riven grinned back.

Matt only meant that he didn't like Stella. And, wow, *agreed.* Finally, a like-minded individual who didn't think the sun shone out of Stella's ass. That questionably located halo was just the effect of the magic Stella was always blazing about the place.

"There's another reason we don't see you around a lot, isn't there?" Matt asked with a grin and a wink. "Seen you sneaking off to the greenhouse at all hours. Meeting someone, obviously. Professor Harvey's little daughter, right?" He scoffed. "Well. Not so little."

Riven stopped smiling.

"Big girls are real eager to please, huh?"

It took Riven a long moment to speak. It felt longer than that, time crushed flat by the pressure of the stone walls. He had to force his fists to uncurl.

"It's not like that, man," said Riven at last.

"Oh." Matt shrugged. "Just in it for the ego boost, then? I get it. Having a girl hang on every word you say is good for the soul. Bet she has a huge crush on you."

Riven mumbled in a vaguely negative fashion, staring out of one narrow, arrow-slit window onto the cobblestones and the lampposts below. Matt nudged him.

"Sure, she does. A cool guy like you, spending time with her when she isn't even able to attend school yet? She must be jumping out of her woolly socks."

"Uh . . . maybe," muttered Riven. "Don't think so . . ."

"I know so," said Matt. "Oh, hey." Another idea seemed to dawn. "Are you in the greenhouse to find, like, *recreational* plants?"

This was better than Matt talking about Terra. Riven shrugged, but let himself smile a sly smile. Matt hooted and buffeted Riven with his shoulder.

"My man!" he exclaimed, throwing an arm around Riven's shoulders. Ilaria returned and snuggled up under Matt's other arm.

When they reached Matt's room, Ilaria and Matt started making out again. They practically fell through the door and onto the bed, kissing wildly. Riven began to edge away. They probably wanted some privacy.

Hair flung out on Matt's pillow, the two of them interestingly tangled up together, Ilaria asked, "Hey, you wanna stay?"

Riven hesitated.

69

Matt burst out laughing. "Wow, that was a joke."

"Right," Riven said. "Obviously. Bye."

Riven left hastily, then made his way out of the Specialists' Hall over to the fancier castle where the fairies lived. He was sick of people like Stella and Sky, fitting into Alfea like hands in gloves, so smugly confident about their place in the world and their life purpose. For a change, he wanted to show the perfect pair they weren't right about everything.

He set out to learn Callum Hunter's and Ms. Dowling's schedules. By Orientation Day, he'd blow this secret romance wide open.

SPECIALIST

Well, that triple date had gone terribly, and now Riven and Stella had a weird bet, Sky thought as he ran his dozen sunset laps around Alfea. Maybe Riven wasn't Ricki's type. He wasn't sure what Ricki's type would be. She seemed to get on well with everyone. She was such a great girl, and so laid back. It was easy to relax in her presence, and Sky didn't let himself relax often.

He couldn't let himself relax now. He was trying to beat his own record for speed. If he did it, he could tell Silva about it. He picked up the pace.

The world was a blur of emerald, the leaves on the trees and the thick carpet of moss on the forest floor mingling together. Deep green alongside deep shadows, and one pale face.

"Oh, hey. Terra, right?"

Once, when Sky had been off with Silva on a mission that ran long, he'd come back and found Terra had shot up and looked really different. He'd blinked uncertainly and said, "Terra, right?" and her brother, Sam, had laughed. So now Sky did it every time. It was a little joke between him and Terra.

Sky stopped in his tracks, coughing in the dust of the road he'd kicked up. "What are you doing hiding out in the woods?"

Terra was wearing a long, faded denim dress and a floral cardigan, and she was half hidden behind a tree. Sky had only seen her because Silva taught him to keep alert at all times.

"Oh!" Terra seemed startled to be seen, and even more startled to be addressed. She tucked some wisps of brown hair nervously behind her ears. "Hello, Sky. I'm here on a nature walk. That makes sense, right? Just noting the new leaves on the trees, and—and spring is a beautiful time, so . . . I love plants. You know that. Everybody knows that! I'm out here because . . . I love plants."

"You love plants," Sky repeated.

Terra's round, worried face disappeared behind her

71

swinging pageboy hair as she nodded vigorously. "I love plants!"

Well, Sky was glad they'd sorted that out. "Okay . . ."

He didn't have much to say about plants. He offered Terra a smile.

"How's training going, Sky?" Terra asked with sudden sharpness. "Kicked a lot of people's asses lately?"

He was no doubt imagining the tone of asperity in her voice. Having lived in Alfea all her life, Terra must be well aware Specialists fought one another constantly. She was just taking an interest. And she wasn't real good with people. Terra tried too hard.

Sky could sympathize. Sky tried hard himself, at a lot of things.

"Not to brag, but yeah, I kick Riven's ass every day," Sky confirmed.

He was about to ask Terra if she was excited about Orientation Day, and starting out at Alfea next year. Except then Terra's eyes, usually sweet and dreamy, narrowed in an alarming fashion. Sky took a step back.

"Wonderful!" declared Terra in a tight voice. "You shouldn't be ashamed of yourself at all!"

"I'm not . . . ?" said Sky.

"Wonderful!" Terra didn't sound as if she meant it this time, either. She spun on her heel and plunged into the shadows of the trees.

That had been a weird interaction, but interactions with Terra often turned weird. Terra was a nice girl, but she was kind of awkward and intense.

Sky shrugged and continued running, falling into a rhythm. Trees one side, gray castle outlined against a sky fading to dark on the other, the Specialists' lakes, mirrors for the darkening sky far away, something in his path . . . Sky twisted and leaped over the vine stretched across the road, then landed neatly and kept running. Silva had left booby traps and obstacles for Sky during training before. Occasionally, also in Sky's bedroom or the bathroom when Sky was growing up. Sky appreciated it. He knew Silva wanted the best for him. Silva wished Sky to be prepared for anything.

Making his circuit around Alfea, Sky saw a figure in dark Specialist gear standing by the lakes. He knew Silva at once from the way he stood, always at attention. Sky permitted himself an indulgence and veered off course, charging over to where Silva was looking into the pewter-colored waters.

"Hey, I cleared your trip hazard," he called as he neared.

"What?" Silva's voice was unusually curt, his chin coming up sharply. Sky felt bad. He'd obviously interrupted Silva when he was deep in thought.

He hesitated, hating the idea of making it worse, but turning and running wasn't a soldier's way.

"Well . . . I decided to run around Alfea twelve times,

because you said my dad ran around the school ten times, and then—"

"You don't have to do something just because your dad did." Silva's voice was as cold as his ice-blue eyes.

What was he supposed to do, then? He wanted to be like his dad. If he was like his dad, then he'd feel closer to him. And . . . Silva had loved his dad. Sky felt very tired suddenly, legs leaden weights from running desperately around school chasing his father.

"No, sir. Sorry, sir."

Soldiers didn't let exhaustion affect them. He gave Silva a nod and turned away, heading back to his run.

"Wait, Sky."

Sky turned.

"Sorry if I was hard on you just now," Silva said gruffly. "Got something on my mind. Of course, I know you want to be like your dad. Of course, you miss having your dad. I'm—I'm sorry."

You just be my dad, Sky thought. He wanted Silva, not some stranger. He didn't miss Andreas of Eraklyon. How could he? He'd never known his dad, hadn't had the chance to.

But that thought was a betrayal, too. His dad hadn't wanted to leave him. His dad would be with Sky if he could.

And he knew Silva would never want to replace Sky's

father. The only reason Silva stuck around was out of duty to Sky's father, the friend he'd loved.

Sometimes Sky wondered if Silva regretted taking Sky in. If it hurt to have a reminder of Andreas, or if it hurt because Silva had hoped Sky would be more like his dad than Sky actually was. If Sky had turned out to be a disappointment.

He could never ask, and he couldn't bother Silva when he was already worried.

"Something on your mind?" he asked. "Anything I can do?"

Silva's face cleared. "Obviously, soldier. Go beat your last speed record."

Sky nodded with fresh determination. "You know it, sir."

He set off. He wouldn't count the last lap of Alfea. He'd start fresh and beat his record. Out of the corner of his eye, he saw Silva square his shoulders and march toward the castle.

He knew his father and Silva had served under a woman commander. He didn't even know the woman's name. He couldn't ask. It hurt Silva to talk about those times. Sky could tell by the way Silva's face closed down whenever Sky asked about the war, or his father.

But Silva did tell Sky what a great warrior Andreas had been. Everybody told Sky stories about Andreas the monster slayer, undefeatable in battle until his last fight. Sky knew his father had been a hero, so his father's commander must have been a hero, too.

That seemed wonderful, to have someone shining to lead the way through doubt, fear, and destruction.

When Sky met Stella, they were both small. Sky felt even smaller than he was in the palace, trailing after Silva as Silva reported to Queen Luna on a mission.

Until he saw how the queen treated her daughter, how small she tried to make Stella, and he wanted to be Stella's defender. He knew she would one day be queen, and he thought she would be a good queen. Sky thought Stella was lovely and fierce and seemed lost. If he helped her find her way, he figured she'd help him to find his.

It hadn't worked out as he'd hoped.

Stella cares more about good lighting than good works, Riven had said. Riven was an ass, but Sky had to admit, Stella kept talking about appearances, about power. She kept sounding more and more like her mother.

He'd never liked Stella's mother.

Sky tried to dismiss those treacherous thoughts. He wanted to be true to Stella.

He loved Stella. He always had. And she needed him. The idea of a shining leader was like the idea of a best friend, a comrade in arms who could always be trusted. They were dreams. Sky couldn't keep chasing dreams.

Sky kept running, under leaves that glowed crimson with sunset as though they were on fire.

LIGHT

It was so lonely in the lightless place. The dark stretched on for miles, like a desert made of night, and despite the dark, she could see how empty this place was. Stella knew nobody would come to save her, that she was trapped forever.

In her tower room, Stella woke screaming.

"No! No, no, no, please, no! Mother, I will be good, I will, I will, I—" Stella realized she was begging out loud and the other girls might hear it through the walls, and what would they think of her then?

Her bedroom, hung with gauzy fabrics and lined with gilt-rimmed mirrors, was blazing brighter than day. Stella buried her face in her hands, curled up in a tight ball in a nest of bedclothes, and shook.

"Stella?" Ricki asked in a small voice behind the door.

"Go away!" Stella snapped, and hated herself when she heard her voice quaver.

The door opened, and Ricki gave a sharp, pained gasp, hand flying up to shield her eyes. Stella hadn't realized before that the light magic, beaming off the walls and refracted by her mirrors, was scalding. She hurriedly quenched it. She intended to quench it utterly, but with tattered memories of her dark nightmare still clinging, she could only manage to dim the magic down until it was a hazy, comforting glow.

"Are you all right?" she asked Ricki quickly, panic rising.

She calmed when Ricki lowered her hands and smiled. "Of course, I'm all right. Stella, are *you* all right? I heard—"

"I don't know what you think you heard," Stella snapped.

"Nothing, nothing," Ricki reassured her. "Nothing I could make out, that is. Only it sounded like you were having a nightmare. I get that way myself when I eat too much cheese in the cafeteria."

Stella smoothed the bedclothes under her hands. They were crumpled like tissues.

"Yes," she agreed faintly. "Maybe it was the cheese."

As if Stella would ever overindulge in dairy products.

"Wanna budge up?" Ricki asked.

When Stella simply stared at her with polite incomprehension, Ricki wandered over in her cheery-red pajamas and patted the mattress. When Stella shifted slightly, Ricki climbed in, pulling the crumpled covers over them both and putting her arm around Stella's waist.

"I hate being alone after a nightmare," she said simply. "Let's have a sleepover."

"It's not necessary," said Stella, then was overcome with the fear Ricki would take Stella at her word and go away. "But . . . thanks. That's thoughtful of you."

"No big deal," Ricki told her.

Long before Stella slept, Ricki's breathing went even and her arm went lax around Stella. The bed was placed under the window, so Stella could see the sky: all the stars like daubs of light magic made by a fairy flying across the dark. Beneath the stars, the green hills around Alfea rolled, deep woods and silver waterfalls, the safest place in the realm of Solaria. Her mother didn't rule here. Ms. Dowling ruled here. Sometimes Ms. Dowling annoyed her mother, and Queen Luna couldn't do a thing about it. Her mother had said once that she wished she could oust Ms. Dowling from Alfea, but here Ms. Dowling stayed. Stella was in awe of anyone who could resist her magnificent mother's will.

Ms. Dowling had never spoken to Stella outside of class, but in class once she'd put a steady hand on Stella's shoulder and talked her through bringing her magic down a notch. "Easy," she'd said, then crisply: "Excellent."

Ms. Dowling wasn't here now. If her mother came . . . but even if Ms. Dowling was here, she couldn't do anything. Nobody could save Stella. Her mother was the adored and all-powerful queen.

The lights in Stella's room leaped and trembled.

In the morning, Stella would slip down to the circle of jagged stones in the woods by the roaring waterfall, where she could replenish her power and be certain to always have light at her fingertips. Stella visited the circle of stones often. Like a maiden waking at the dawn of a spring day to wash her face in morning dew so she would stay beautiful, except this was about staying powerful.

Then she'd get ready for Orientation Day, to execute her splendid plan.

Stella patted Ricki's arm, as her own heart stopped beating too fast beneath her silk and lace nightgown. She felt composure settle over her, until she could be a princess sleeping serene, and finally let her eyes fall closed.

Her last thought was that she hoped Ms. Dowling would come back to Alfea soon.

MIND

Musa turned the pamphlet for prospective students of Alfea over and over in her hands. She was tempted to crumple up the paper, but she didn't. Orientation Day was very soon now, and she still hadn't made up her mind.

"What do you think, Mom?" she asked aloud to the still night air. "Should I go? Or should I turn this into a paper airplane?"

As a Mind Fairy, Musa didn't believe that the dead lingered on and listened to the living. She could reach out with her power and experience people's thoughts and feelings. That meant she could reach out with her power and experience the hollow where someone's mind and heart used to be. Her mother wasn't a lingering benevolent presence. Her mother wasn't looking down on her from above. Her mom was *gone*.

So Musa wouldn't visit a grave, or keep ashes, or any of

that. She knew better. But sometimes, she slid on her headphones and played the rock she and her mom used to blast, windows open, singing along as they drove.

Her mom had been alive once. She'd loved Musa once. Musa had felt it. When she played the music, she could remember how love felt.

Musa walked alone, as was her way, listening to her music and talking to her dead mom. She didn't have anyone else to talk to about this invitation to school in Solaria. She probably wouldn't go. She didn't see the point. Schools were full of people. Musa didn't do well with people.

She took another peek at the pamphlet.

The pictures made the school look like a castle. Like a fortress, which would keep anybody inside it safe. Musa longed for safety, but walls wouldn't help her. And they wouldn't help the people trapped inside those walls with her, either. Musa could vividly imagine the horror that would be, to have a bunch of students feeling hostile about her, listening to them think that they didn't want Musa reading their thoughts.

She didn't need to improve her powers. They were plenty strong as they were. Of course, if there was someone at Alfea who could help her make other people's thoughts *less* intrusive, that would be different.

That didn't seem likely, and even if it was true, what would be the cost for help? Musa wouldn't get her hopes up. Hope was for suckers.

Her own powers hadn't been any help when her mother was suffering. Musa was with her when she died. She'd felt the death as if it was her own. Musa had tried to help her mother, but she hadn't been able to take enough of her mother's pain away. She'd broken down, she'd failed, and the memory of her failure and the echo of her mom's tortured, dying thoughts would never leave her. Even now, when she tried to imagine what her mom would advise her to do, she could only hear her mother's silent screams.

With trembling hands, Musa turned her music up. Before, when she played music this loud, she'd dance to it. That was when her mom was alive to watch her dance, and Musa could feel the shimmer of her mom's pride as well as her own happiness. She was done with hope. She was done with dancing.

That left the question of what Musa *could* do. She was coming up empty, and then this pamphlet had arrived like an answer when she didn't have any.

Going to look at Alfea was different from committing herself to attending. Surely, a single visit couldn't hurt.

She walked aimlessly down a path, kicking stones out of her way with her combat boots, trying to seem as if she knew where she was going.

Musa didn't have anything better to do. She might as well check out Alfea.

THE HEART
GROWS OLD

Saúl Silva found the headmistress's chambers dark and echoing with emptiness.

Farah hadn't come home to Alfea yet. He didn't know where she was. Ben said she'd left a message, saying she would be back in time for Orientation Day. Silva didn't know why Farah hadn't left a message for *him*.

Her absence unsettled him deeply. He always wanted to be sure where Farah was, ever since they were a team of young, fearless warriors against the Burned Ones, since they were the unstoppable strike force. Rosalind gave the orders, but before Saúl could launch into battle, he always had to check on his team.

Is Andreas beside me? Is Ben backing us up? Is Farah ahead?

Saúl and Andreas always walked together, Saúl just a step behind Andreas. Farah was always in sight, and he always followed her. He still had that, though when he looked to his brother-in-arms now, Andreas wasn't there. Would never be there again. And it was Saúl's fault.

He crushed down that thought with brutal, military efficiency. He looked around the chamber for another moment, at the circular window with its green-and-blue-and-yellow stained glass, casting undersea light that poured out onto the rows upon rows of old books Farah loved. There was a spiral staircase that led to even more books. Rosalind used to be headmistress here, but Farah had made this room her own.

He might be the headmaster of the Specialists' Hall, but the way Silva saw it, the Specialists' Hall was simply part of Alfea. Ultimately, Farah Dowling was in charge, and that was the way he liked it. At heart, Saúl Silva would always be a soldier, looking to his general for orders.

He didn't hesitate to give Farah his opinions, but he trusted Farah to steer their course. He'd had a general once who gave the wrong orders, but that was long ago. Rosalind was in the past, and he didn't let himself think of her. Farah had never led him astray. Silva often went on missions, but Farah stayed at Alfea. She was the fixed point of the world.

When she was gone, he was leaderless. He had to choose his own fate. It made Silva remember doubt, bringing him back to the day when he had to choose between Rosalind's orders and what he knew Farah would think of those orders. He'd chosen Farah.

His best friend had chosen Rosalind.

His thoughts were straying wildly tonight.

He left abruptly, turning on his heel and making his way down the broad flight of steps in the hall and outside into the courtyard. But he didn't head for the Specialists' Hall. Instead he went toward the greenhouse, where there was a light shining.

Inside the greenhouse, strange plants were flourishing, some safe beneath the glass and some sweeping up the sandstone walls. Ben Harvey was at one of his lab tables, crouched over an experiment. At the sight of him, the tension in Silva's shoulders eased slightly. One of his teammates was still here. Ben was the smartest man Silva knew. He could rely on Ben with absolute faith. He trusted this brilliant man to find a solution to anything.

"What's up, nerd?" said Silva.

Ben raised an eyebrow but didn't lift his eyes from his experiment. "Saúl. I'd ask what brings you here, but I'm pretty sure I know."

"Where is she?"

"No idea," said Ben. "But her note said she was going to investigate something, and I wasn't to worry."

"That's worrying."

Ben nodded. "Before that, she asked me for a potion that traced any kind of magic. Rather a tricky thing to make, fascinating actually—"

"Not to me," Silva said firmly.

He appreciated Ben's genius, but he wasn't able to understand it, and he didn't try to do useless things. His philosophy was simple. Geniuses provided solutions, leaders planned out a means of using those solutions, and Silva accomplished the mission.

"Yes, well, you philistine." Ben sighed, every inch weary Professor Harvey. There were elbow patches on the man's cardigan, and he was totally out of shape. Sad. "Normally, such a nebulous potion wouldn't do much good, since magic is all around us. So this suggests to me Farah wasn't sure what she was looking for, and she was searching for it in a place where there wasn't much magic."

"The human world?"

Silva frowned. Farah shouldn't go to the First World. He didn't like the sound of that place. The kids often talked about it, because they looked up things on the internet. Silva felt there were many better uses of magic than the internet. Apparently, the human world had the internet, too, though it didn't work by magic there.

"It's an interesting place, Saúl."

"Sky shows me pictures from the human world sometimes," Silva said. "I don't like it. I don't like Instagram. Riven told Sky to get one. That boy is a bad influence."

"I have an Instagram," said Ben cheerfully. "It has many pictures of astonishing plants in it. Terra and I follow each other. She's a wonder with the filters. Makes the plants look superb on her Instagram, bless her."

"I'm sorry to hear that."

He wouldn't have thought Terra would waste her time with useless things. Terra was a lovely girl. She and Silva hadn't spoken much, which suited Silva. She was shy, Ben said. Silva understood that: Silva was shy himself, though he'd never told anybody that as it was nobody's business but his own. Still, he'd noted that Terra's earth magic had many uses for battle. She could strangle or bind people with vines, slip the ground out from under them or bury them deep, and Silva suspected she'd do it without flinching. Ben's earth magic was less ferocious, and his boy Sam's was used mostly for retreat and reconnaissance and more peaceful still, but Terra Harvey was going to be a killer. Silva had big plans for her. She'd be excellent to have on the field with a Specialist team beside her, once she was trained up.

"I've seen posts about you on Instagram," Ben said. "Dreadful posts. The kids call them thirst traps."

"What," said Silva, in flat horror.

"Hashtag silver fox fairies."

"I'm not a fairy!" Silva snarled. "And I'm *not* going gray."

"Just a little," teased Ben. "Around the temples. Farah can handle herself, you know. No need to fret."

It wasn't like Farah to disappear off somewhere, certainly not in search of mysterious magic. It made Silva think of the one thing that never failed to unsettle Farah. *Rosalind.*

"I'm not fretting," said Silva. "Idiot. She should have sent me. That's all." She should know that he would do whatever she asked.

Ben softened, eyeing Silva with concern as though Silva were some babe in arms. "Perhaps she didn't want to worry either one of us. Or for either one of us to go. We have our kids now."

"Sky's *not* my son," Silva snapped.

Ben was no help. Silva left the greenhouse, slamming the door on the way out. He shouldn't have bothered coming. He and Ben were still a team, of course, but Ben had drifted far away in spirit if not in fact. Ben had buried the soldier he used to be deep, and now he pretended he was gone. Ben wore cardigans as though he'd never worn armor, and had family dinners at home. He and Silva didn't understand each other, and Silva couldn't explain himself.

Words were Farah's domain, complicated and terrible in a way swords weren't. Silva wasn't able to talk about what was in his heart, not even to Ben or to Sky. It had always been a relief to him that Farah was a Mind Fairy. She must know how he felt, and they never had to talk about it.

If there was one thing Silva was certain of, besides Farah, it was this: Saúl Silva knew perfectly well that Sky wasn't his son.

Silva didn't deserve to be his father.

He wasn't like Ben, couldn't do cardigans or dinners. He'd never meant to keep Sky. Even before Andreas died, he hadn't visited Sky enough. Silva had got into the habit of dropping by to see the baby, bring Sky toys and listen to his earnestly incoherent babble. After Andreas was dead, Saúl went one final time. He'd needed to look in on Sky, needed to do that much for Andreas. So he'd gone for his last visit, and Sky had lifted his eyes to Silva's face and taken what the nurse said were his first steps. Toward Silva, tottering but determined. He'd picked up Sky with his rough battle-scarred hands that had no business holding innocent children. Only a year old, with golden curls and steadfast eyes.

Sky. Saúl hadn't been able to work out letting go of him. So he'd taken Sky along. He'd carved Sky wooden daggers, and later swords, and even when he was still baby-small, Sky's grip on the hilt was steady.

"You'll always look out for him, won't you?" Andreas had asked on one of Andreas's increasingly rare visits home, when Sky was a baby in the cradle, rolling about and laughing and eating his own impossibly small feet. "Like you do for me."

"I promise," Silva said. He'd stabbed Sky's father through the chest less than a year later.

Andreas, Saúl thought to himself sometimes. *You would be so proud of him. Almost as proud as I am.*

Even Andreas couldn't be as proud as Saúl was. Nobody could be as proud of Sky as Saúl was.

Over the years, Silva had gone on many Specialist

missions by himself or with a team. He always took Sky with him. Sky should get used to soldiering life young.

There was never any question Sky was a born soldier. Silva had guided his baby steps toward an armory, had seen baby Sky try to lift a sword bigger than he was. It was Silva's task to make sure that Sky fought for a just cause and the right reasons.

When he was on the road, or in Queen Luna's palace, he kept Sky close.

Sometimes the dreams came of war long past—one night he dreamed of the Blackwoods Massacre, and another night of the battle by the waterfall and the bodies in the river. On the worst nights, he dreamed of the worst day and the worst battle, of blood in the grass and the burned-out shells of those houses, of Farah crying and Andreas dying. Silva would wake from those dreams shuddering and moaning like a man gutted. Then he would rise, wash his face in cold water in a brook or one of Luna's beaten-gold sinks—it made little difference to Silva—and allow himself to look in on Sky. He could find a measure of peace in watching the child. Sky slept peacefully in a bedroll or in palatial splendor, disturbed by no horrors and no guilt.

My good little soldier, my best boy with your clear eyes and sure aim and your clean warrior's heart. What would you think of me if I told you how filthy that heroes' war you admire really was? Will you hate me? Will you turn away?

Of course, Sky would.

In Sky's mind, Silva and Andreas were perfect heroes. Sky didn't know that the past seemed golden to him because he was looking at it in the reflection of his own golden heart.

One day, he would know. One day, Sky would know everything. Silva knew he owed Sky the truth. When he told Sky, he'd make it clear that none of it was Farah's fault. Silva was the one who made the choice, who drew the sword. It was all Silva's fault.

Silva didn't want to go back to his chambers, which were simple and always ready for packing up, and empty. He returned to the Specialists' lakes. There was no harm getting some practice in. Every year that passed, he recovered from wounds more slowly, and his muscles and joints ached more. Age came hard to those who had lived hard, and he had to keep up with the youngsters he was training. If he failed, somebody else might get hurt.

He got his broadsword and went through passes, trying to force his mind to think of the methodical patterns and nothing more.

Peace was difficult to come by when a man was made for war. He missed being able to look in on Sky, now that Sky was living with the other students in the hall, roommates with that boy Riven, whose reflexes were good but whose eyes were shifty as shivering sand.

Some might say Riven thought too much, but soldiers thought plenty. Soldiers weren't stupid. Still, Riven *did* think too much, in one way . . . in the wrong way. His challenges and questions came at the wrong times, and never came at the right ones. He was the type who would pipe up uselessly just before a charge, or build up a challenge too big in his own mind and shrink at the worst possible moment.

Silva didn't want anything holding Sky back. He worried enough about that girl, Princess Stella. He'd been pleased seeing them together at first—of course, only a princess could be good enough for Sky—and the girl's light magic was tiger strong. But Stella's control was awful, and she wasn't improving. She was getting worse. One day, she was going to slip. She might be a liability rather than a help in battle, and she might turn out too much like her mother, after all.

Sky was too good for them both, too good for this world. Sky was wise and kindhearted, an Andreas whom Rosalind had never touched.

Sky would never follow a false leader the way Silva had, for as long as Silva had. Silva had been the one who discovered Rosalind's plan to destroy a whole village with dark magic. Rosalind had promised Farah and Ben that she'd evacuated Aster Dell, that there were only monsters left, but it wasn't true. Later, Farah said they had to pay for what they'd done. They had to be the ones to stop Rosalind.

Saúl, are you with me? she'd asked him.

Silva said, *To the death.*

Only they had lived. Silva was a soldier. He'd been fully prepared to die. He often thought he hadn't been prepared to live.

To live on somehow, to do his duty, after that day. When Silva had to go tell Farah about Rosalind's plots and lies, and Andreas had stood in his way. His best and dearest friend, his comrade in arms, the man Silva would have gladly laid down his life for. It always came down to this: Silva had chosen to follow Farah, and Andreas had chosen to follow Rosalind.

So Silva had drawn his blade and killed Andreas. Before that day, he'd kept a kill count for men and monsters both. For the first time in his career, he hadn't confirmed the kill, hadn't closed Andreas's eyes and paid him the last tribute of a brave fight well fought. There hadn't been time. There had been so much blood. Silva had slipped in his best friend's blood on the stained grass as he ran to help Farah and save Aster Dell.

Only he was too late. The village was already in ruins, nothing but blackened walls on the side of a mountain. There were the frames of houses exposed like skeletons, and there was no soul left alive, and there was a baby shoe lying in the ashes, blackened and curled up like a dead leaf by flame. It was the only time he'd ever seen Farah cry.

Silva couldn't make up for those twin disloyalties: following Rosalind to disaster, and killing Andreas to try and stop it.

Andreas. Silva saw his face in so many nightmares. His best friend. Sky's father.

Silva still remembered how Andreas was, at school and after. The hero of Eraklyon, a one-man army who killed more monsters than anybody else. Everyone, men and women alike, admired him. Nobody else ever measured up, ever talked like him, looked like him, fought like him. Andreas was everybody's choice, every time. Silva understood completely. There had never been any question between Andreas and Saúl who was the better man.

War changed them all. Silva told Sky stories about Andreas's prowess in battle, but he didn't want to tell Sky how bloodshed twisted and changed Andreas, how Andreas got swept away with battle fury and liked it too much. Their own soldiers were scared of Andreas near the end. Silva did what he could for them, but how could anyone be reassured with their shining leader stained and only Silva to turn to?

Sky was like Andreas, but not in that way. Sky had always been kind. Nobody taught him that. Sky came up with it on his own. Every day, Silva told himself Sky could never change as Andreas did.

Before the wars, Silva was different, too. He laughed easily back then. He was the one who started the tradition of the Senior Specialists' party in the abandoned East Wing, him and Andreas and Farah and Ben laughing and drinking and dancing among the relics of old wars. Until Silva became a relic of war himself.

Blood changed the earth when enough was spilled. A battlefield could never be simply a field again. Silva wasn't surprised that some dark magic of Rosalind's might have risen. He wouldn't be surprised, even if he saw one of the Burned Ones come running at him again in all its monstrous fury. Peace never lasted. War always came back.

It was up to Silva to be ready with sword and shield.

One day, the long shadow of their sins would come for them. Silva was prepared, and he'd made sure Sky was prepared. To fight. To defend Farah and Alfea. Silva wouldn't let what he cared for most be dragged down into the bloodstained mud.

Not my leader. Not my boy. Not while Silva had breath in his body and a sword in his hands.

When Andreas was alive, joy was easier. Even though joy was harder now, it still happened. Joy was Sky's face, was getting the chance to love him for at least a little while longer. A soldier's life was a lonely one, but there was honor in that. If Silva was truly honorable, he'd be even more lonely. Instead he leaned too much on Farah, when she had so many burdens. He pretended, to himself and Sky, that he deserved Sky's affection.

If he died for Farah or Sky or for Alfea, his endless guilt would finally be over, and his sins washed away. Silva didn't fear death. He only feared not being there when what he lived to defend was in danger.

And that was another lie. He feared, too, how Sky would look at him once the boy knew the truth. He had never been able to tell Sky what he had done. He'd tried and frozen up, cold and stern, a thousand times.

Your father's blood is on my hands, but I held on to you. I'm a killer, and so was he, and I took him from you, and I can never replace him or make up for all I have done.

In the end, Silva was the worst thing a soldier could be. Silva was a coward.

Exhausted, he sat down in the long grass by the lakes at dawn, leaned his broadsword on his knees, and rested his forehead against the cold, clean blade.

Where was Farah? If only she would come home, and command him again.

Fairy Tale #3

What could have made her peaceful with a mind

That nobleness made simple as a fire . . .

—*W. B. Yeats*

THE HEART
GROWS OLD

The human world was a place apart, where magic was not born. Magic hadn't even crossed over to this place, not since the practice of leaving changelings here was abandoned. Farah stepped out of a portal inscribed on the air and gazed around at where Rosalind's letter had led her.

This place had arid desert air and silver rows of cars as far as the eye could see. California, the mortals called it. The magic of the fairy realms made machines less necessary for daily life, and technology magic handled what was required. Farah was used to stretches of woodland, the crash of waterfalls, and the crackling presence of the Barrier. The Barrier was invisible until something or someone touched it, and then rippled out into the air with blue and purple shimmers. The magic of the Otherworld was very different from the traffic lights and neon signs of this world.

Ben had made Farah a potion from roots that would trace any magic in this Californian air, a vial of shimmering filaments reminiscent of iron filings. When she twisted the stopper free, she spilled the silver out upon the wind.

Faint and luminescent as the track of some invisible snail, the potion traced a path upon the sky. Farah followed its lead down a narrow street crowded with small shops. She studied a storefront of strange perfumes, one claiming to smell like sugary cereal and one like a camel.

If such perfumes were a type of magic, Farah wanted nothing to do with it. She marched on, then hesitated at another store, a little antique shop. The silvery trail hunting magic seemed to wink into starry life around the brass bell hanging from the flaking green surface of the door.

An antiques store might be the ideal place to hide a magical artifact. Hesitantly, feeling as nervous as she used to when approaching Rosalind, Farah pushed the door open.

Inside were tottering heaps of junk covered with a layer of dust like high mountains under deep snow. Any dangerous and powerful magical object hidden here was certainly well concealed.

In the dusty air, the magic trail gleamed, almost disappearing into darkness and emerging again as a sharp glint in a corner stacked with debris. Farah followed the trail to discover the silver magic curling around a sorry-looking broken lamp, its stained-glass lampshade encrusted with grime and tilting madly to one side.

That couldn't be the treasure. Farah approached, walking softly, wondering if she might glean some useful information by speaking with the storekeeper. Farah wasn't prejudiced against humans as some were—her secretary was human—but someone from this world wasn't likely to know anything related to Rosalind. Still, she had no better plan.

The sound of raised voices and hurrying footsteps outside stayed her step.

The door burst open with a rattle and a jingle of bells. Farah receded into the shadows, waiting for the human customers to go about their business.

"Come on, Mom, come on, come on," said a girl with long rippling red hair, charging in. "Come see the coolest lamp ever."

The woman at the girl's side was blonde and very well put together, but had the harried air of someone whose life plan and ivory pants hadn't included stores full of dusty junk.

"Bloom," she said, "were you out combing through junkyards and antique stores all last weekend?"

"Uh, no, Mom," the redhead told her. "I was home all day Sunday fixing my new clock."

There was a touch of wry humor in the woman's voice. "Perhaps I'd know you were in all day Sunday if you'd opened your door, or deigned to speak to me or your father . . ."

"Mom!"

"It's not that I object to you being out," said the mother. "Socializing is great. If you were out with your friends—"

"What friends?" said the girl. "Everyone at school thinks I'm a weirdo."

"And why is that?"

"Because I'm kind of weird?" offered the redhead.

The girl seemed fine to Farah. Pretty name, Bloom. Old-fashioned. Farah had no time for the way parents these days named their children peculiar, newfangled names like Chad or Karen.

The pair fell into a clearly often-aired argument, the edges of their sentences so well-worn that they overlapped easily.

"If you gave people a chance to get to know you—"

"—happy the way I am—"

"—leave your room—"

"—hey, you could be thankful I'm not racing stolen cars with hot boys—"

"—at least eat dinner with us—"

"*Mom!*"

A high, squeaky chime sounded as an inner door scraped open. A man with an air of authority was ushering another woman out. This woman stumbled as she went, and only then did Farah notice the woman's eyes were so filled with tears she could barely see.

"I would've thought they were worth more," she said. "They're pieces of my past. I hated to sell them, but we could really use the money—"

"Nah, practically worthless," the man assured her. "I'm doing you a favor taking them, since I knew your dad."

There were two china figurines under his arm. The woman gave them a longing, uncertain look, but the store-keeper's air of certainty obviously had her cowed.

"Wait," said the girl, Bloom. Her voice was suddenly ringing, and furious.

"Bloom, hush." The woman took her daughter's arm and drew her back.

"You don't get it, Mom," Bloom hissed, turning to her mother. The other woman seized her chance to escape, fleeing out the door with a mumbled thanks, and Bloom whirled around. "Those are Dresden figurines!" she snapped. "They're worth a *lot*."

The storekeeper blinked. "They're fakes. Sorry to disappoint."

Indignation enveloped Bloom's face like fire swallowing a forest. "I don't think so. That's not fair! You cheated that woman."

Her fury seemed to fill that dim room heaped with dusty junk, its brightness calling gleams out of tarnished metal.

When Bloom moved forward, the storekeeper took a step back. Farah Dowling, who rather liked to see a girl with a will of her own, smiled thinly.

Bloom stormed forward another step, the air practically crackling around her, but her mother caught her arm. "Don't make a scene, Bloom. Go wait in the car."

Bloom stared, hotly betrayed. "You're not fair, either!"

She turned on the heel of a low-heeled boot and bolted out the door, hair trailing out behind her like a banner, the bell ringing behind her like an alarm.

Her mother sighed. "Sorry about that."

"She's got a smart mouth," the storekeeper said.

"She's passionate about justice," her mother corrected, eyes narrowing. "Sometimes she can be rash, and I apologize for that, but it's not a bad thing." Her eyes traveled to the grimy lamp. "How much for that? She seemed to really like it. Said it was a find."

"It certainly is, Ms. Peters!"

The storekeeper, all charm now that a sale was in view, sold her the lamp. Eventually, the mother followed her daughter out the door.

Ms. Dowling's urge to seek the storekeeper's assistance had faded, and when she took out Ben's vial, the trail had faded, too. Farah knew the lamp had no magical properties—she was powerful enough herself to be absolutely certain of that.

Yet the silvery particles now floated aimlessly like bright dust blown about. As though some magic treasure had whirled through this place, but not stayed.

There was a mystery here, but she couldn't linger in the human world too long. Her friends would be worried, and Alfea needed her. She had an Orientation Day to attend.

SPECIALIST

"Come on, Riven," urged Sky. Stella had strong ideas about punctuality, and if they didn't leave the hall now, they were gonna be late to help with the setup for Orientation Day.

Riven was lying in bed with his leather jacket on and his head turned to the side, jaw at a super weird angle as he took a picture with his phone.

"I'm constructing the perfect thirst trap," he claimed.

Right, the picture was for his Instagram. Riven had bothered Sky into getting Instagram, and Sky didn't fully understand it. Stella selected approved couple photos for Sky to put up. Sometimes Sky took pictures of nice views or nice swords and posted them. Silva twitched whenever the word *Instagram* was spoken.

Sky lived in fear of the day Riven said something like "thirst trap" in front of Silva. It would not go over well.

A happy thought occurred to him. "A thirst trap for Ricki?"

Riven cackled like an evil fairy. It was unsettling. Sky didn't see what Riven thought was so funny about the idea of dating Ricki. He thought any guy would be lucky to date Ricki.

"Nah. Just, you know. My many admirers. Various stalkers. You know how it is."

"Not really," said Sky. "I don't think I'd like being stalked. Terra Harvey almost gave me a heart attack slinking through the woods yesterday."

Finally, Riven was ready to move. He must have realized that they were running late, too, because he practically sprang out of bed and stormed down the steps on his way out of the Specialists' Hall, taking several at a time. For once, Sky had to hurry to catch up.

"Terra wasn't stalking you," Riven snapped at Sky once he'd caught up.

Riven snapping at Sky wasn't an unusual occurrence, but a certain note in his voice gave Sky pause. "Do you know Terra at all?"

"Um . . . don't think so," mumbled Riven.

"She's Sam Harvey's little sister."

"Sam Harvey is a loser."

"Sam and Terra are Professor Harvey's kids. You like Professor Harvey. You like his lectures."

"No, I don't," said Riven, scowling at the ivy on the courtyard walls. "I don't remember his lectures. And I don't like anyone."

Professor Harvey had actually seemed impressed with Riven's way around a laboratory. He'd said that Riven had the best pipette technique of any Specialist he'd ever seen. Then Mikey and the others had started teasing Riven for being a nerd, and Riven had flushed dark red and gone angrily silent. Sky couldn't believe Riven had forgotten all that.

Sky was actually starting to get a bit concerned. "Riven, did you hit your head?"

"I don't have to hit my head to think the way you assume everybody worships you is sickening," Riven spit out.

Sky took a step back, alarmed by his vehemence.

"I don't think everyone worships me," he said slowly. "Terra was just on a nature walk when I ran into her. I only meant it was startling—"

Matt joined them, carrying a load of posters under his arm. "Terra Harvey?" he asked. "Oh, is it *you* she's into, Sky?"

Sky flashed back to Terra's venomous glare at him yesterday. "Definitely not."

"Absolutely not!" Riven agreed.

Sky gave Matt a suspicious look. He didn't like the way Matt had talked about several of the girls, and he'd seen Matt checking out Terra as she bustled by carrying

107

plants for her dad. He wondered if he should give Sam a heads-up about Matt. He'd want to know, if it was his sister.

"I guess you've got your hands full with Stella," said Matt. "Speaking of having your hands full, take these. She gave them to me along with some very specific orders I didn't listen to. Who died and made her the boss of everybody?"

Riven smirked.

Behind Matt, Stella said: "Do what I say, and nobody has to die. Unless you're volunteering for death?"

Sky smirked. Stella pushed Matt so he stood aside, and she was revealed, standing tall with her hair in another high braid. She gave Matt a glittering, dangerous smile and pointed to the wall.

"Decorate efficiently," she commanded in a sweet voice, "or face the consequences."

Matt slunk away obediently and got a ladder. Stella zipped about, rounding up the committee like a stern golden sheepdog, ordering ribbons and bunting hung. Ilaria was an Air Fairy, so she could make stuff float before Sky jumped up and pinned it.

"Riven, are you thinking about vandalizing our 'Welcome to Alfea' posters?" Sky asked.

"Er," said Riven.

He was already in the middle of scrawling on the poster so that it read "Welcome to Hellfea." Sky sighed and rubbed at the picture with the edge of his sweater sleeve, until Riven's scrawled words were blotted out.

"Riven, stop vandalizing our 'Welcome to Alfea' posters."

"Buzzkill," grumbled Riven, but he kept putting up the posters, even when Stella had gone away to command Ricki and Ilaria—whereas Matt slunk off immediately.

Riven was weirdly reliable sometimes. Sky gave him a grateful grin. Seeming vaguely surprised, Riven grinned back.

When she returned, the sound of her high-heeled boots like crossbow bolts striking home, Stella's voice rang against the stone walls. "Where did Matt go?"

Maybe Riven was simply staying put out of self-preservation. Sky shrugged apologetically.

Stella's voice was menacing. "He will pay for this later. But I need you now."

Sky began to climb down the ladder.

"Not you," said Stella. "Riven." She went over to where Riven stood, waving a paintbrush covered in glue as if trying to ward her off.

"Our love can never be," Riven told her. ". . . Because I don't like you."

"That's so tragic, when I have such a thing for scruffy losers with inferiority complexes and chips the size of the castle on their shoulders," Stella shot back. She dragged Riven away by the sleeve of his leather jacket.

Sky shrugged and began walking around the inside of the castle, armed with posters for plausible deniability. He put one poster up here or there, in places he felt fit the bill for what Stella had extensively described as well lit and appropriate. But mostly Sky was looking around for someone who frequently used his earth magic to disappear through walls. Sam was the retiring type.

Sky had never felt as comfortable in the castle as he was in the Specialists' Hall. It was beautiful here, even before Stella had adorned the walls with her sparkling, living lights. The glass of the balcony rail was painted with flower petals, and affixed to the stone walls were swords and shields hanging up pointlessly rather than being used in war, and torches with stylized copper flames bursting from them, brilliant but with no warmth. Sky would have preferred real fire.

The delicate stone arches and stained glass that made the place lovely also made it seem unfit for a soldier. As a kid, Sky had been concerned about smashing one of the windows or harming one of the flowers in the greenhouse. He felt worried for fragile things, but he never found anything truly beautiful unless it was strong.

At last he saw a glimpse of green and found Sam Harvey carrying a fairy girl's books through the corridor overlooking the balcony. Sam was telling the girl a joke in a low voice, but she seemed distracted by something as Sky approached.

"Hey, Sam," Sky said. "Can I have a word?"

Sam's brown eyes widened.

"Wow, Sam!" exclaimed the girl. "Are you friends with *Sky*?"

Sam's eyes took on a focus usually seen in starving puppies. "Er . . . well, yeah . . ." Sam mumbled.

"Totally," confirmed Sky. "Friends, very much, yes. Hi. Are you Sam's girlfriend?"

"Oh, no." Sam sounded shy.

The girl tossed her black hair. "You never know your luck, Sam. Maybe we could have a double date with you and Stella, Sky . . ."

"Sounds fun," said Sky politely. "We just need a minute in private. Really sorry to ask."

"It's no problem, Sky!" The girl took her books and skipped off, apparently in a state of high excitement.

In contrast, Sam seemed weirdly deflated as he watched her go.

"What's wrong?" Sky asked.

They went to sit together on a low dark wood bench, Sam huddled a bit into his worn green jacket. Sky used to see him and Terra gardening outside when they were kids, Terra in a smock and a cardigan, Sam in his green jacket and little red cap. Sam and Terra had always looked like a set. A family unit, perfectly peaceful and happy in their union. Sky couldn't intrude.

"Nothing, really." Sam sounded sad. "Thanks for backing

me up there. I kind of liked her, and I was hoping to impress her a little. But she was a lot too impressed. No offense, Sky, but I'd rather a girl's favorite thing about me was *me*, and not just something I can do for her. Know what I mean?"

"I think so," said Sky. Sam was very low-key and didn't show it off much, but he was a pretty smart guy.

Sam shrugged. "Ah, well. There'll be other, cooler girls. Can I help you with something? Can't imagine that I could, but . . ."

"No, I'm good."

"I figured."

Sky came out and said it. "This is about Terra. There's this Specialist guy Matt who's kind of a creep about girls, and he mentioned her today. I didn't love it. Just wanted to give you a heads-up."

Sam was silent for a minute, freckled face screwed up in thought. Sky hoped he hadn't come off as a creep himself, warning someone to guard the womenfolk. Maybe he should've talked to Terra herself rather than her brother, but he knew Sam a little better because of being the same age. Creeps were an awkward thing to bring up.

"Thanks," Sam said at last. "Good of you to tell me, since we're not really friends. You're a good guy. I mean, everybody knows that."

It was a compliment, not an insult, even if it sat weirdly with Sky. All he could say was "Thanks."

Sam was frowning now. "You think this guy's been bothering her?"

"I don't know. Wouldn't you know? You guys are always together."

Sam's frown went deeper. "Not so much lately. I've been busy with school, meeting new people, and Terra's—well, you know. She can be a lot. For new people."

Sky was silent. He'd heard that if you didn't have anything nice to say, you shouldn't say anything at all.

"Hey," said Sam, "I'm not like you, okay?"

That struck Sky as mean. He might expect Riven to say something like this, but not Sam. They weren't friends, but he'd never known Sam to be cruel.

"Right, you're not," snapped Sky. "If I had a little sister, I'd want her with me all the time. But unlike you, I don't have a family."

He got up from the bench and walked away quickly. The lights from the oriel windows of the castle went by in a blur, and soon he was going down the wide flight of stairs into the entrance hall. The doors of the castle were transparent as windows, and the green-helmed, arched windows in the hall were big as doors, streaming sunlight winking against hanging brass light fixtures. Woodland rolled behind the glass, promising escape.

"Wait," Sam yelled after him, thundering down the steps in Sky's wake.

Sky turned and waited for him. Sam had to pause to breathe, sink down on a step, and mutter that Specialists went too fast.

"Wow, that was *not* what I meant," said Sam once he got his breath back. "I meant that you're, like . . . effortlessly cool and popular."

"Okay, whatever," said Sky. "The other thing matters more, don't you think?"

"Yeah," Sam muttered. "I know it does. Sorry if I was a jerk."

They were silent for a moment. When conversations got awkward, Sky never really knew what to say. Usually in the bad silences, he and Silva would go and have a match with the staffs, the crossbow, or the sword.

Sam probably didn't want to do that.

"It's cool," Sky muttered back.

Sam nodded. "Thanks again for the heads-up, man."

That was that. Sam, who believed Sky led an effortless life, clearly didn't have anything further to say to him. Sky's eye fell on the slightly vandalized "Welcome to Alfea" poster that Riven had hung up alongside the ivy growing along the walls. At least Riven always had something to say.

"No problem," Sky told Sam. "Later."

He jogged down to the foot of the stairs, and then instead of escaping, he walked the halls and put up the rest of the posters for Orientation Day. He should try to help out. Stella was counting on him, and Sky never wanted to let anybody down.

LIGHT

Stella had to admit delinquency had *some* uses. Riven had provided her with a detailed account of Ms. Dowling's and her secretary's schedules, and now they were acting on it. As she supervised the decoration of the school, Stella had taken a detour to Callum's desk and seen it empty at a time it shouldn't be. Perhaps it was nothing. Possibly Callum was simply trying to take advantage of Ms. Dowling's absence. Riven had reported Ms. Dowling took thirty minutes for lunch, and her assistant got only fifteen, which wasn't long enough for even a substantial sandwich.

But perhaps it was something.

She'd brought Riven along to investigate this matter. She might be caught while looking into this unsavory business. If Stella was going down, she wasn't going down alone. She was absolutely dragging Riven and his filthy mind down with her.

As they climbed the narrow stone steps toward Ms. Dowling's office, Stella decided they should consult. "If someone finds us sneaking around, we should have a story prepared."

Riven hesitated. "The most believable reason for a guy and a girl to be creeping off somewhere by themselves is if they're looking for a hidden place to make out." He sounded very reluctant to offer this theory.

There was an appalled pause as they both absorbed the implications of this. Riven had pulled up the hood of his hoodie, Stella noticed, as if this would make him more difficult to spot. Stella hadn't mocked Riven yet, even though Riven deserved mockery, because the hood did make it more difficult to see his face and that was a personal bonus for Stella.

"That's true," said Stella at length. "But I would rather die than have anyone believe that about us."

"Hard same," Riven agreed. "Let's say we were sneaking off to duel."

"Fine," Stella told him. "If anyone asks, I won."

"Why do you get to win?"

Stella gave him a dazzling smile. "I'm just trying to make the story believable, Riven!"

She swept on ahead, heading up the retinue as a princess should. Riven snorted and shambled after her.

They found Callum's desk still abandoned. Stella and Riven lurked by the gray filing cabinet and exchanged a glance. Stella refused to admit it, but she was uncertain how to proceed.

"Maybe Callum's delayed. Maybe he's puking in the bathroom," suggested Riven. "Could've eaten a bad toad-stool. Humans are sensitive." He paused. "Or maybe he's wildly making out with Ms. Dowling in her office right now."

Stella gave a thin shriek of protest. "You vulgar, foul-mouthed cretin, he is not! She's probably not even back yet!"

Riven shrugged. "Only one way to find out."

Despite his big talk, Stella noticed that Riven made absolutely no move toward the headmistress's office. Once again, royalty had to lead the way. Girls were doing it for themselves, because men were basically useless.

Stella lifted her chin, stepped up, and pushed the heavy carved door open. She and Riven advanced in through the door. They saw Callum, his curly head bent over the contents of Ms. Dowling's desk as he went through her papers, pen flying rapidly over a page.

When Callum looked up, there was an expression of absolute guilt on his face.

They stopped dead on the threshold. Riven made a startled grab for Stella's jacket. Stella shook him irritably off—her jacket was pristine houndstooth—and smiled innocently at Callum.

"Oh no, I'm sorry," Stella said in her airy voice that meant "I don't actually have to be sorry; I'm a princess." "We accidentally stumbled into the office while we were looking for a place to—"

"Make out," said Riven, clearly panicking.

"*Duel!*" exclaimed Stella, and glowered at Riven. "To the death!"

"Right, totally," said Riven. "Wait, to the what now?"

Stella and Riven exchanged glares that indicated they were disappointed in each other as conspirators. Then Stella crossed the floor toward Ms. Dowling's broad mahogany desk. The circular window above the desk was a mosaic of multicolored glass, a circular swirl of green and blue and yellow. It was very beautiful and created an aquamarine low light in which it was difficult to scrutinize documents from a distance.

"May I ask why you are in Ms. Dowling's office?" Stella asked. "Didn't she leave it locked?"

Callum hastily folded up the piece of paper. "Obviously, as her secretary, I have a key. Don't hurl accusations at me. Your mother may be the ruler of Solaria, but Ms. Dowling is the authority at Alfea, and you're a student here before you are a princess. You two are trespassing."

Stella advanced upon the desk, hoping to get a glimpse of what Callum had been writing or any of the other papers laid out on the surface of the desk. A globe was blocking her line of sight.

With a firmness surprising in one with such a weak chin, Callum escorted Stella and Riven out of Ms. Dowling's office. Stella and Riven went silently down the stone steps until they could be sure that they wouldn't be overheard, then turned to each other.

"Did you see his face?" Riven hissed. "Guilty as sin!"

"Callum always looks guilty. It's because he resembles a ginger dachshund in corduroy," Stella said impatiently.

"Guiltier than usual!"

Riven might have a point there.

"I agree his behavior is very suspicious," conceded Stella, "but that means nothing. Maybe he's doing evil. Maybe he's stealing from her!"

If he was, Callum should be thrown in prison. Could a princess perform a citizen's arrest?

"She gave him a key," pointed out Riven. "He was writing her a secret love note to hide away in her desk. It's obvious."

What was obvious was that Riven was a secret soppy romantic. Stella hoped Ricki would enjoy this trait of his. Personally, it made Stella feel physically unwell. They walked along the corridor slowly, each lost in thought. Below, over the balcony rail, Stella could see the students of Alfea wandering under her Orientation Day banners and ribbons.

"We need to settle this business once and for all. Until we see them together in a scenario that might lend itself to romance, this is speculation."

Riven was scowling. "How are Ms. Dowling and Callum gonna find themselves in some random romantic scenario?"

"Leave that to me," Stella said serenely. "See you tomorrow."

She was an accomplished lady. She could plan eight-course meals and say "Do you have that in a size four?" in ten languages. This would be a snap.

"See you tomorrow, Princess," said Riven. "Get ready to lose your light show."

Stella gave him a dramatic eye roll and braid toss. It was more than Riven deserved.

As she descended the broad staircase alone, she used her magic for a trial run for the light magic she'd set, in an intricately thought-out pattern, around the castle. Light flared with her steps, her braid bounced with each jaunty stride, and people made sounds of hushed awe that followed her as though her every step had an adoring echo.

Silver was on the tree. Gold was set in the curved windows, as though stars had flown down to perch on the windowpanes. Magic was laid upon the ground outside like snow made of frozen light instead of frozen water. The light filling the arched windows with radiance threw the shadows of surrounding branches across the stone floor, so their castle seemed surrounded by an enchanted hedge. On the final step of the stairs, Stella activated the magic she'd tucked away beneath every step. Power flared and turned the staircase into a cascade of radiance, a lightfall of radiant foam she'd just emerged from. Stella held her head high, limned by ferocious luminosity.

People started to clap, the applause rising to the high vaulted ceiling. Some shaded their eyes with their hands, but Stella told herself firmly that they were saluting their princess.

All around, Alfea glowed, and it was down to Stella.

Lights, camera, action. The scene was set for Orientation Day.

The future was glorious.

WATER

Trying to change up her style for Orientation Day had been a mistake. It looked as though Aisha had murdered a mermaid in her bathroom.

In retrospect, Aisha didn't have great luck with bathrooms. She had flashbacks to the incident with overflowing toilets at her last school.

Now that it was too late, Aisha could admit there'd been a certain amount of panic involved in her decision-making. She'd told herself she was finally going to Alfea, where she'd learn to be a boss with her magic. It was the perfect time to streak her box braids with cobalt blue just as she'd always intended to and always chickened out of actually doing. People often seemed surprised that Aisha was into flowing dresses and jewelry and makeup as well as intensely into sports, and she'd felt a little self-conscious adding a new hair look to the mix. But even though Aisha worried about other people's expectations of her, she believed in doing what she wanted.

She got the bottle and went to work.

An hour later, she was gazing at her own reflection in horror. When it became clear matters were going wrong, she'd tried to absorb the moisture of the dye back out with her magic. Since the dye was mostly dry and her powers weren't the most reliable—not yet!—this had only created a terrible neon-blue patchwork effect.

"You ready for the Orientation Day at Alfea?" her coach had asked her earlier.

"You know me, Coach!" she'd chirped. "Born ready."

Aisha wasn't sure she was ready for Orientation Day at all.

No. Aisha leaned forward, and made eye contact with the girl in the mirror. She focused determinedly on her eyes, not her hair. She instructed herself to be sensible. *You can do this, sport.*

Winning was all about attitude. Aisha wanted this to go well, so she had to believe it would. Nerves lost as many competitions as lack of skill. She couldn't psych herself out. She didn't need to be ready for a leadership role yet. Nobody would make any huge demands of Aisha tomorrow.

Orientation Day was an introductory day for future students, intended to show them the ropes of the school. This was a simple training session, getting Aisha prepared for life at Alfea.

Aisha pointed to herself sternly in the mirror. "Get your head in the game."

What could go wrong?

EARTH

Tomorrow was Orientation Day! Terra was unspeakably excited. Tomorrow she'd probably meet her best friend! Or, you know, she wasn't picky. If they had a group and everybody liked one another an equal amount, that would be fun, too. They could have communal sleepovers in the common room of their suite, and a blanket fort, and gossip about boys! Or if one of her besties wanted to gossip about girls, Terra would be there for them. She was so ready to be a supportive bestie.

She mustn't get ahead of herself. Tonight was going to be awesome, too. Dad was trusting her with something huge. She couldn't wait to show Riven.

She was humming as she made her way to the greenhouse with a chest full of freshly washed vials in her arms. She took the long way around to visit with her plant friends: past the ground-crawling strawberry tree, under the purple beech, linden, and larch. She checked in on the Specialists' lakes, but the training grounds were deserted, the calm water a mirror to the evening sky.

"How are you doing, Ter?" asked Sam, falling into step with her.

The mere sight of her brother made her angry. She never got to see him these days. He didn't even eat with her and Dad anymore.

"Oh, I'm fine," Terra assured him in a brittle voice. "Very busy. Like you're busy, with all your new friends."

She wasn't going to cut Sam slack just because he'd finally remembered that he had a sister. She marched along the gravel.

"There's this Specialist guy . . ." said Sam.

"What Specialist?" exclaimed Terra.

She wasn't a gifted con artist. Her brother gave her a weird look. Terra had to admit, that was fair.

"Oookay," said Sam. "So, maybe you've noticed him hanging around—"

"I don't know him!" Terra insisted.

"He's a big guy in second year called Matt," continued Sam.

"Oh," said Terra. "Oh, I actually don't know him." That sounded extremely suspicious, even to her. "I don't know anybody," she added firmly. "How could I know people at Alfea? It's not like you've been introducing me to your friends."

Sam seemed knocked off course. "Hey, that's not what this is about."

"What is it about, then, Sam?"

Sam stared at her helplessly.

"Like I said," Terra told him, "I'm busy. Now if you'll excuse me, I have to go meet someone who actually *wants* to spend time with me."

She left her brother standing in the sunken garden and hurried for the shelter of the Osmanthus, breathing in the scent of jasmine to calm herself. She checked in on the flowers as if she was nodding to acquaintances of long standing, though she couldn't stop for them. Speedwell, daisies, rhododendrons, and elderflowers in a burst of pink lace, like the dress of a girl attending a long-awaited party.

She was so mad at Sam. Her brother, who saved earthworms with her when it was raining or the sun was shining too fiercely. Her brother, who was kind to everybody but who hadn't been kind to her. Sam was annoying, and she hated him.

When Terra opened the greenhouse door, Riven was already there waiting for her. His head was cradled in his arms.

Terra hastily set down the chest on the lab table and rushed over to him. She patted him on the head. Riven looked up, blinking sadly.

"Did something terrible happen?" Terra asked sympathetically.

"Yeah, I had to spend an hour in Stella's company."

"Wow!"

Terra was so impressed.

Riven gave her an accusing glare. "No. Not wow."

"Gosh, I think Stella is wonderful," said Terra. "In a scary way. Very, very scary. But she's so gorgeous and impressive, don't you think?"

Riven made a face. "I think she's a splitting headache in human form."

"Oh," said Terra, startled. "I would've thought any guy would like Stella. Since she's, well, as beautiful as the sun."

Riven snorted. "Yeah, look at that too long and it'll turn you blind."

"Has Stella been bullying you as well?"

"What do you mean, as well?" Riven snapped. "Nobody's been bullying me."

"Of course, of course," Terra soothed. She knew she had to be careful with Riven's touchy pride. "I'm sure Stella is horrible."

She gazed around the greenhouse for inspiration to cheer Riven up, and her eye fell on the truthbell crates.

"So, were you, like . . ." Riven seemed to be searching for words. "Hanging around Sky yesterday?"

Terra bit her lip. "Oh, he noticed that, did he?"

Riven seemed thunderstruck. "So you were!"

"Oh, gosh," Terra said, distressed. "Yes? I suppose I was."

She couldn't lie. She highly disapproved of lies. You didn't lie to people, especially not if they mattered. Lying wasn't for buddies.

"Do you have," Riven said between his teeth, "a crush on him, or something?"

It was Terra's turn to be thunderstruck.

"On Sky?!" She began to laugh. "That's hilarious."

Had Riven not noticed that Sky's hair looked very strange sometimes? It fell into odd shapes. If Sky was a plant, Terra would've wondered what was wrong with his petal formation. Plus, whenever Sky saw Terra, he said, "Terra, right?" They'd known each other their whole lives, but Sky wasn't sure about Terra's name. Terra understood that Sky was cool and everything, but she had her pride.

"Yes, that is hilarious, isn't it?" Riven sounded calmer. "Uh—is it? Why is it? I figured that Sky was the kind of guy that, uh, any girl would like."

"The way Stella is for guys?"

Riven seemed horrified by this point of view. "Wow, Terra, no. Sky doesn't give the impression he eats people's heads after they get down."

"That's true," Terra admitted. "Sky *is* less scary than Stella. Sky can cut you with his sword, but Stella can cut you with her words, which I think is far worse. Also she can flambé you with light magic and possibly have you executed. Can she have people executed? She's a princess, so I feel like maybe she could. I'm talking too much," Terra concluded. "I know I'm talking too much."

Sometimes her train of thought escaped from her, careening wildly out of control across the conversational landscape. Especially when she was feeling anxious or excited. Terra was always well aware when it happened, but she always *became* aware far too late, after she'd already made a fool of herself.

Riven shook his head. "You're fine."

His voice was gentler than usual. He really didn't seem to be annoyed by her. Terra thought she could trust that.

Riven tended to make it extremely clear when he was bothered by anything.

"I suppose Sky is handsome," Terra continued, considering the matter as Riven scowled, "but he's not very *appealing*, I don't think."

Riven brightened. "You're so right, Ter."

She couldn't imagine Sky needing to be taken care of. He was a shining hero type, unapproachable as a marble wall. Also, anyone even dreaming of approaching him would have to deal with Stella, and that would obviously spell death.

Terra wasn't interested in courting death. She *was* interested in romance, but she'd always figured it would happen once she started attending Alfea properly. That was when she'd get friends, and a boyfriend. That was when her whole life would begin.

She'd decided she was like a plant, waiting for the right time to bloom. Plants were deeply romantic—suitors gave people roses. A lot of flowers had love names, like forget-me-not and love-in-idleness. And of course, flowers were useful for making love potions. People talked about planting kisses, and they didn't just mean her dad planting a gentle kiss on her head when Terra was stooped over a microscope in the greenhouse or in her bed falling to sleep. They meant, like, *plant one on her.* What was planted needed to be watered and nurtured. Terra had big plans for her first kiss.

Someday, love would blossom for her. She'd meet a super nice boy and she'd just know he was the one.

Until then, it was a little uncomfortable to think about. Terra's dad said she was a late bloomer, but she hadn't been physically. She'd been thirteen when she heard a couple of Specialist guys comment on her body. One of them had been approving, and one of them hadn't been, and Terra couldn't decide which repelled her more. She knew how guys talked about girls like her.

She'd want her boyfriend to be very sweet and kind, and never say anything mean about anyone. Never even *think* anything mean about Terra. She wanted him to think she was great. And maybe even, if it was at all possible, beautiful.

Riven sounded puzzled. "So why *were* you following Sky around?"

Terra was happy to clear up the confusion. "I was following Sky around to trip him up with vines! Because he bothers you at lessons. He vaulted over the vine, but I'm evolving a different plan."

Riven's face went blank. "You're evolving a what now?"

"A scheme of vengeance!"

"Oh, a scheme of vengeance," Riven said faintly.

"I'm not on Sky's side," Terra assured Riven. "I'm on *your* side."

Riven kept looking oddly startled, but his mouth tugged out of its usual sulky-to-neutral shape into his rare brief smile at that.

"So do you have . . ." Riven began. "I heard someone say a funny thing. Maybe you'd think it was funny, too. Do you have a huge . . . ?"

Terra stared in utter confusion. She had no idea what Riven was getting at.

Silence reigned among the hothouse plants.

"Never mind," said Riven. "It's not important. Hey, some of these plants could be used for . . . amusing purposes, right?"

"Do you mean they're funny shapes?"

Obviously, Terra had gone to many markets with her father to buy fruits from goblin men. There was always a vegetable stall, and at the vegetable stall there was always a vegetable someone made an unsavory joke about. Terra had heard the humans wrote poems about fairy fruit, but she hadn't heard of anyone writing poems about humorous fairy vegetables.

Riven coughed. "No, I mean like . . . recreational, hallucinogenic purposes."

"Riven!"

Terra was scandalized. Then she wondered if that was desperately uncool. Riven was a year older than her, and he'd even gone to the Senior Specialists' party, though he'd spent the rest of the weekend curled up in the greenhouse under her grandma's knitted blanket as she brought him herbal teas. The Senior Specialists' party seemed wild.

"I mean—oh, you," said Terra, and flapped a hand against his arm, trying to be relaxed. "I mean . . . there *are* plants like that in the greenhouse. And if you really wanted, I could— But shouldn't you think twice before, like, haha, just as an example, wrecking your future by continually getting high? Wouldn't that be a disgusting waste of your potential, which would break the hearts of everyone who cares about you? Haha. Just throwing around possibilities here. I'm cool. I'm relaxed. I'm *chillaxed*, in fact. Haha."

Riven gave Terra a look that made her fear she hadn't been entirely chill.

After a moment, he asked in a careful voice, "You think I have potential?"

"So much!" Terra enthused. "Of course, I make a special effort to watch your and Sky's matches whenever I can."

Riven's eyes went wide. "Oh no."

"You have such good reflexes!" Terra assured him. "You learn everything Sky teaches you really fast! Faster than any of the other Specialists, I think. Of course, if you slow your reflexes and ransom your future because of peer pressure and a wish for passing amusement, then—"

"Okay, okay." Riven started laughing. "Just say no to recreational plants. I got it. Don't scheme vengeance against me. You terror."

"You terror" wasn't a nice thing to say to someone,

but the way Riven said it was nice. He sounded almost impressed by Terra being a terror. He wasn't, of course, but it was fun to pretend.

"I'm really looking forward to Orientation Day," she confided.

She wished she could ask Riven to stick beside her, and make her look cool to the fairies she was hoping would be her best friends, but she knew she couldn't.

"Stella's gonna make it weird," Riven predicted. "She's deeply unhinged."

Terra patted him some more. Sometimes she feared Riven had a very dark view of the world. She nodded at nearby ferns, and the ferns reached out leaves to pat Riven as well. The patting would continue until Riven's morale improved.

She offered an alternate viewpoint. "I think Orientation Day is going to be great. And you know what else? The truthbells are blooming tonight, and Dad trusted me to collect the pollen! You can help me," she added, glad to give Riven a treat since he seemed to be having a trying day.

She entrusted Riven with a vial and went over to the crate, removing the lid she'd pried off one last time and setting the flowers around them in a silver circle as they waited for the time, which was exactly when the last star winked into sight over Alfea.

On the last star the truthbells bloomed, filmy petals unfolding from their little stone pots, like beautiful veiled women emerging from a dozen wells. The pollen rose from the flowers' hearts in bright fountains, spilling tiny dancing truthbell seeds out upon the air. The flowers were that dark silvery color, but the seeds were flame and cobalt and ochre and jade and sparks of sunshine, painting the air in jewel tones. The truthbells made a sound like tiny bells, too, ringing to acclaim the truth. Terra laughed in delight and lifted two vials up high, whirling in dizzy joy with her face uplifted and electric rainbow shades playing against her closed eyelids. These plants had grown in what other people thought of as dirt and dark, yet now truth was beauty, and beauty was truth.

Terra spun to face Riven, glowing. "Isn't this the coolest and prettiest thing you ever saw?!"

He was watching her twirl and smiling again, that hard-to-catch smile, but this time the smile stayed. Caught, like a flower that could be pressed in a book to keep.

"Yeah," Riven agreed, softly. "It's not the worst."

MIND

Now that they were on the way, Musa was gloomily convinced Orientation Day at Alfea would be a bust. She huddled in her purple jacket and wondered why she'd bothered to come.

The coach that was bringing the future students to Alfea was pumpkin colored. It wasn't pumpkin shaped, it was shaped like a regular school bus, but Musa wondered if that was how the stories got started about how you traveled to the magic castle.

Her eyes skipped over the other inhabitants of the pumpkin-colored coach. Musa hadn't been this close to this many people in a while, entirely on purpose, and the proximity was disorienting. There was a girl with blue in her black box braids, which was very cool, but under the funky blue and black Musa could sense driven purpose and frantic worry. Musa bounced off that mind into an auburn-haired, dark-eyed girl thinking about secrets, and then turned hurriedly away. Musa didn't want anything to do with any secrets. A boy with buzzed hair was staring out the window, thinking about fear, panic, and—more secrets?

She didn't think any of the other potential students were Mind Fairies like her. Musa raised her eyebrows to her reflection in the window. She was the only person in the know. Was there nobody on board the school bus who didn't have a dark secret?

Probably not. People were like that—guilty. Musa knew she was.

Musa preferred to travel alone, but here she was bottled up with everyone else on this long drive past the cliffsides and through the woodland.

If crowds were a forest, Musa was a fenced-in tree, protected by wire. The other trees might try to get in at her,
poking her with their branches through the wire, annoying
her with the ceaseless rustle of their leaves, but she didn't
have to be part of the forest. She chose not to be.

She'd try out this school so she could learn to fence herself in better, but she wasn't interested in getting to know
people. Musa wanted everyone at a distance, where it was
safest. For them and her.

She and her mother used to take road trips together,
singing along to classic rock, but Musa wouldn't think
about her mother anymore. She slid on her headphones and
let the music drown out all thought, even her own. Music
was her only comfort. Sometimes it felt like magic far more
than Musa's mind-reading abilities. That ability felt more like
a curse.

The furious beat of the music soothed her, and she got
lost in the rhythm as she tapped her fingers against the
glass. Then the coach turned on the winding road around
the high granite mountains studded with trees, and Musa
saw Alfea laid out before her.

She'd read the pamphlets. She knew what to expect. And
Musa wasn't usually easy to impress.

Under what was still a cold, starry sky, there were deep,
dark woods, with the magical Barrier hidden among the
pines and oaks, and fir trees that framed the moon as it paled

in the lightening sky, and a castle that seemed more like a sprawling fortress. Alfea looked magical, but far better than magical, it looked remote. Far away from bustling streets, busy minds, and pain.

Alfea might offer a possibility of peace. It had been a long time since Musa felt peaceful.

THE HEART
GROWS OLD

The day was dying in the human world. The red line on the horizon, like blood brimming at the lip of a chalice, was not caused by the sinking sun alone. Palm trees and white towers were touched by the reflected light of real flame.

Farah had read there were frequent fires in California, so she paid the skyline little attention. Even if she had been watching, there would have been no way for her to tell that the fire was born in a small antiques store where a woman had been cheated that day.

Weary after her fruitless search, the headmistress of Alfea turned her back on the fires and departed for the fairy realms.

DO MOST BITTER WRONG

Dear Sir,

I'm afraid I must report that some of the Alfea students are suspicious of me. I had taken advantage of Dowling's absence to go through her secret papers and was copying them for you when Princess Stella and a Specialist boy, who I believe is Sky's roommate, abruptly entered the chamber and interrupted me. They made very unconvincing excuses about why they were here. I saw right through them at once.

I have not been informed that the princess is aware of our dealings with the palace, so she may be acting on behalf of others.

It is very unfortunate and I know will be corrected someday, but for now Sky is fanatically loyal to Specialist Headmaster Silva, and Silva is Dowling's creature. It's imperative that I find out what these two spying children think they know.

Fortunately, a truth potion has been harvested and made from fresh truthbells by Professor Harvey this very evening. It won't be hard to obtain the potion and dose the snoops.

~~And you say I never take initiative.~~

Yours respectfully,

Callum Hunter

138

Fairy Tale #4

O you will take whatever's offered
And dream that all the world's a friend,
Suffer as your mother suffered,
Be as broken in the end.

—W. B. Yeats

SPECIALIST

Sky ran a circuit of Alfea at sunrise on the morning of Orientation Day, as he did every day. He liked those bright, quiet times, when the sunrise hit the cliffs but not the deep, dark woods, and the path ahead was clear.

When he got back, Professor Harvey was waiting for him outside the Specialists' Hall with a cardboard tray of coffee in paper to-go cups. You could get coffee from the cafeteria, but only at certain times, and this was far too early. Plus, when Sky peeked under a lid, there was cream and cinnamon.

"Word came from Ms. Dowling," said Professor Harvey. "She's on her way back. She wanted to send along this little token of appreciation for you kids—the committee, I think Callum said? Since you did such good work setting up for Orientation Day when Ms. Dowling was called away."

Sky grinned. "Cool. Thanks, Professor Harvey."

The professor handed over the coffees and ruffled Sky's hair so it fell into his eyes, as Sky's hair always seemed to wish to do. Sky's hair refused to be as disciplined as the rest of him. Professor Harvey was super nice, a comfortable sort of dad in his worn checked-flannel shirts. Sky thought Sam and Terra were lucky to have him.

Sky ran up the stairs of the hall and into his room, humming. He put the coffees down on the big desk under the window, between his and Riven's beds.

141

"Wstfgl," said Riven, emerging from a tangled nest of blankets. "For me?"

"Coffee?"

"For me," Riven insisted, grasping at air.

Sky took pity on him and put a coffee in his hand. Riven took a deep swallow of the coffee. Sky got changed, combed his hair so it wouldn't fall into his eyes, and grabbed his own coffee. Maybe Professor Harvey or Ms. Dowling would tell Silva they thought Sky'd done a good job with the committee for Orientation Day. Silva would be pleased Ms. Dowling was coming back. Silva might be pleased with Sky.

"Why do you even bother combing your hair?" Riven asked. "It looks better getting right out of bed than mine looks after an hour trying to get it into a just-out-of-bed style."

"Uh," said Sky, startled. Riven seemed slightly startled himself.

That was a nice thing to say, though? Sky nodded acknowledgment and gave Riven a small grin. It wasn't like he didn't know Riven spent time on how he looked. Tragically, Sky was around for all the shirt-open selfies Riven intended for Instagram.

"Come on, we gotta get going," Sky urged. "Stella will want us to make things perfect. She always wants perfection, and I always feel like I'm not meeting her high expectations. But then, that's how I always feel, anyway."

Riven choked on his coffee.

"Wow, I'm getting ready, I won't be late! There's no need to lay this heavy a guilt trip on me!"

Sky hadn't meant to lay a guilt trip on Riven. In fact, he'd never meant to say any of that. He frowned down at his coffee.

Riven pulled on his leather jacket over his hoodie, giving Sky a freaked-out side-eye. They met Stella in the courtyard. At this point Stella and Riven had a shorthand for their mutual distaste, giving each other fractional sneers with noses wrinkling and mouths pursing, but only for a flicker of an instant before they proceeded with their lives.

Sky gave Stella her coffee and a kiss.

"You're so pretty," he told her. "I always thought if I could save the princess, that would make me a hero. But I'm starting to believe you don't want me to save you."

Stella's crystal-blue eyes went questioningly to Riven, who shrugged.

"I don't know why he's talking this way. Guess his mind broke under the pressure of dating you. Can't blame the man. And like, yeah, he's not wrong—you're hot and everything, but the sequins make my eyes hurt. Also you're a scary lunatic."

Stella's mom wore a bunch of sparkly stuff, too. He guessed Queen Luna could be Stella's style icon and not her role model, but Sky still worried. He found himself wanting to say so. It was surprisingly difficult to keep his mouth closed.

"It's not my problem if you don't understand high fashion, Riven," snapped Stella. "Anyway, this isn't my official Orientation Day outfit. I change my outfit at least twice a day to keep things fresh for photo opportunities. And you seem to own only one pair of sweaty jeans; we are not the same."

She reached out with her free hand and slid it up Sky's back, proprietarily.

"You can't have a spiral of self-doubt about not deserving me on Orientation Day, Sky. I don't have time to deal with it. You're the cutest guy in Alfea, not that you have much competition. Congratulations. You get the princess!"

She skirted around one of the low benches and imperiously indicated a banner that had come loose from a pillar.

"Condolences, you get the princess," Riven muttered, and went wearily to fix the banner under her supervision.

Sky leaned a hand against the wall. "Does anyone else feel . . . kind of weird?"

"Nope, I feel completely normal," said Riven.

"I don't feel normal—" said Stella.

"There's a surprise—" said Riven.

"—I feel totally focused on Orientation Day!" Stella chirped. "Excuse me, I have to go try on my official outfit and do my hair. I hope I can trust you to put the finishing touches on our efforts. I rely on you completely, Sky. If you ever stopped being dependable, I don't know what I would do. Riven, I hope someday you fall off one of your sparring

144

platforms and drown in the lakes so Sky can get a better friend."

Riven saluted Stella with his coffee cup. Stella waved at Sky and went back up the stairs.

"Let me help you with that banner," said Sky, pulling himself together and using his height to get the banner fixed in place.

Riven snorted and left Sky to it. "Always showing off."

"I'm not showing off," Sky said, hurt. "I'm just trying to do my best, Riv."

He jumped off the bench and landed beside Riven, who took a step back.

"Yeah, maybe. Looks like showing off to everyone else. Hey, I always wondered. Why do you call me Riv? Sorry if you think all names should be one syllable, *Sky*, but my name only has two syllables. Can you just not be bothered saying the whole thing?"

Things definitely felt weird. Sky frowned, trying to think his way past the confusion. Something was off, but he couldn't tell what. All he could fix on was his strong urge to tell the truth, but that wasn't wrong.

Blinking, he said, "I call you Riv because we're friends."

"Friends?" repeated Riven. The note of cynical disbelief in his voice was obviously genuine. "You're always showing me up and beating me up."

He was not! He'd seen Riven, who was smaller and kind of weedy, and wanted to take him under his wing. He'd tried to do the right thing, and once again, apparently, he'd failed.

"I—" said Sky. "No, I'm trying to *help* you—"

"I don't see it that way. I've never once thought of you as a friend."

Riven's lip curled, and his eyes were cold. Sky was aware that Riven sometimes said stuff he didn't mean.

He was under the strong impression that this, Riven meant.

Sky always wanted to help, but apparently, he hadn't been helping.

"I should go," he mumbled, and headed for the Specialists' lakes, for consolation and for Silva.

He found Silva there, as Silva so often was, more comfortable on the training grounds than he was in his bare, severe bedroom. Silva was squinting at the light magic daubs that had been placed at strategic intervals around the lakes, making the water sparkle as though it was a mirror for stars even during the day.

"Your Stella is, uh, certainly committed to sparkle action," Silva observed as Sky approached.

"Fairies are supposed to make the world better," said Sky. "Isn't that why we fight to protect them? What's the point of struggling unless the world gets better?"

Silva's eyes flared, blue beacons of disapproval, then his jaw set with the resolve to pretend Sky hadn't said any of that useless stuff.

"Right," he announced crisply. "Sounds like you could use

146

a training bout before we do all this pointless Orientation Day business."

"Why is it pointless?" Sky asked. "Stella's worked hard to make the day beautiful. I've done my best to help her. Why not show people that they're welcome at Alfea?"

Rather than answering right away, Silva took up a staff and scowled at him. Every conversation they had ended in a battle, one way or the other.

"I show them they're welcome by showing them how to fight," Silva answered shortly. "Your father—"

Sky exploded. "Oh, my father! 'Your father, he was such a fighter, he died fighting.' That's all you ever say about him, that he fought. Why do you never tell me the real things?"

Corners of Silva's mouth jerked down sharply. Such a sign of displeasure would've usually made Sky take a step back, pretend his questions didn't matter, but somehow he couldn't pretend today.

"Why do you never say what really matters?" Sky clarified.

"What's realer than war and death?" Silva grated out.

They were standing facing each other as if they were about to fight. A serious fight, a fight that wouldn't stop until someone bled.

"Did you care about him?" Sky demanded. "Do you care about me?"

He caught himself before he said *love*. He could never mention love to Silva. He'd cut his tongue out first.

This was bad enough.

"Sky!" Silva exclaimed, sounding shocked.

He had to stop. Silva would be so disappointed in him for this.

"I care about you," Sky burst out desperately. "That's why I asked you if I could call you my dad, when I was little, but you didn't let me—I don't know if you even *want* me—"

Silva's face was pale. "You're not well. Let's get you to Professor Harvey."

No. He couldn't stay with Silva, or he'd say more terrible things. Sky didn't regret them yet, but he knew with distant dread that would surely catch up with him soon, that he would. What if he could never look Silva in the face again? What if Silva wished he'd left Sky behind in Eraklyon?

Silva had raised him to be a brave warrior, but this morning, Sky turned and ran. He went faster than he'd ever gone trying to break speed records for Silva, down the tree-lined avenue and past the sleek orange-tinted bus carrying the prospective students coming to attend Orientation Day.

WATER

The white boy who was bombing past Aisha's window, fair hair flattened in the wind, was going faster than the bus. He must be a Specialist.

"Whoa, I can't run like that," muttered the guy across the aisle from her.

Aisha raised an eyebrow at him in friendly inquiry. "Specialist?"

He gave her an apologetic little smile, white teeth flashing. "Supposedly. I'm not sure."

Aisha nodded sympathetically. "I've heard the training's rough."

The smile disappeared. "That's not what I'm unsure about," he said distantly.

"I'm Aisha, by the way."

"Dane," he muttered, but she'd already lost him. He'd turned his head, black hair buzzed short, back toward the window.

She couldn't blame him. Aisha looked, too, and was thoroughly distracted by the sight of the gates of Alfea, flung open to receive them.

The gates themselves were black iron, golden leaves curling into a fretwork of ebony-painted thorns. Set over the gates was a large golden *A*, with crossed swords intricately woven in and behind the emblem for Alfea. The bus reached the end of the long, tree-lined avenue and passed through the black-and-gold gates.

There was a gravel drive in a sinuous shape, leading up to a great gray edifice with towers and pinnacles. There were so many different types of windows—casement windows and gable windows and oriel windows, arrow slits and embrasures—that must let all different shapes of sun-light in. The bus rounded the circle of grass in the gravel driveway and stopped before the doors of Alfea.

They climbed out of the bus, into a courtyard with black iron lampposts and green ivy running up the gray walls. On the balcony over the huge doors there was an unfurled golden flag. Aisha couldn't see the symbols on the flag, because affixed to the flag was a sign reading in bright flowing script: *WELCOME TO ALFEA!*

Someone very extra was at work here.

Aisha and the others climbed out of the bus and stood facing Alfea. The school was sprawling, like a whole country encased in stone. Its mountains were towers and chimney stacks, its lakes wide windows. Aisha felt very small look-ing up at the castle.

Two men stood in front of the open entryway doors, under a light fixture shaped like a lantern. One was bald, wearing a tweed jacket with elbow patches over a flannel shirt, and peering at them all with mild, kind eyes behind round glasses. The other man, with very direct blue eyes and very short dark hair that had the appearance of being hastily sleeked down, wore all black and gave the impres-sion that he was bristling even while standing at attention.

"Hello, hello," said the man with glasses. "I'm Professor Harvey, and this is Specialist Headmaster Silva."

The man in black nodded curtly and looked away, as

though he found an introduction an embarrassingly personal interaction.

Professor Harvey kept talking, but everyone's eyes had moved past him to the sight over his shoulder. Including Aisha's.

Beyond the flung-open doors there was a hall, and a flight of stairs that lit up now like a galaxy being born. Down the starry steps came a girl wearing a silk suit that was all bronze and peach, the colors of clouds at dawn. Her blonde french braid was intertwined with a gold ribbon. When she reached the foot of the stairs, flanked on either side by stone wyverns, she spread her arms wide as though to display the school or simply display herself. There was a big gold ring, its complex design shimmering with magic, on one hand.

Aisha suspected she'd found the mind behind the glittering welcome sign.

LIGHT

Stella reached the foot of the stairs, wrapped in both light magic and sunlight, and found a gaggle of Orientation Day kids gathered together at the doors with their mouths open. She fully understood. They must be completely overwhelmed.

"Welcome to Alfea," Stella said in her most gracious tones, descending on a girl with the most lost and timorous expression, and a truly unfortunate outfit. "I can see you need guidance. Let me show you the school."

There was a peculiar pause.

"I know my way around Alfea," said the girl. "I live here, Stella."

Stella frowned. "You do?"

"I'm Terra Harvey," said the girl. "Professor Harvey's daughter? I've lived here my whole life. We've spoken before."

"I don't recall," Stella murmured. "And you'd think I would remember someone with such tragic taste in clothing."

Terra's eyes went wide and stricken. She needn't do an impression of a wounded deer. If Stella didn't provide honest feedback, Terra couldn't work on herself! Still, perhaps Stella had been too harsh. She wanted everybody to enjoy Orientation Day.

"I make my own clothes," Terra whispered.

"Maybe this outfit is an anomaly for you," Stella said generously. "Maybe this is the only floral print in your wardrobe."

Terra's lip wobbled. "I love flowers. I mean, doesn't everybody love flowers? They're beautiful, as well as useful. Just the other day we got a shipment of truthbells to the greenhouse that bloomed last night, and I was given permission to collect the pollen myself. The vials have to be carefully stoppered to stop truth escaping. The cycle of the truthbell is actually very interesting—"

Stella felt forced to interrupt. "No, no, it isn't. You're badly mistaken, deeply boring, and you need to be quiet now. Enjoy orientation!"

She waved Terra firmly away, then looked around for someone more useful and less talkative. She'd had an Earth Fairy in mind for her plan, but now that she thought about it, she didn't think Light and Earth were a great combination. A Water Fairy would be far more suitable. Or perhaps an Air Fairy. There were many possibilities.

Stella's eyes combed the crowd, and she found the three most likely possibilities among the new fairies.

There was a girl in a flowing purple-and-blue midi dress, peacock colors flattering against her dark skin, and a denim jacket too casual for Stella's tastes. Her hair was blue in patches. Stella didn't fully understand her alternative hairstyle, but she was pretty certain she knew what the blue meant. Water Fairy.

"Name?" she asked.

"Aisha," said the Water Fairy.

Stella considered the second possibility. This girl had sallow skin, a cleft chin, and sparkly, shifty eyes. She was twisting air absently around her fingers, wearing a plaid skirt, and had a lot of nerdy chic. She looked as if she knew how to handle herself.

"Name?" she asked the Air Fairy.

The girl saluted mockingly. "Beatrix, ma'am! Reporting for duty, ma'am!"

No, Stella decided to discard the second possibility. This girl Beatrix's attitude reminded her unpleasantly of Riven.

Stella examined the third possibility. This girl was olive-skinned and short, bristling inside a puffy purple bomber jacket like an angry little hedgehog. She had peculiar hair, but it suited her somehow. Stella couldn't get a handle on what kind of fairy she was, but the mystery was intriguing.

"What's your name?" she asked with a gracious smile.

"Musa," said Musa the mystery fairy, giving Stella a disturbingly sharp glance, and Stella took an involuntary step back. She didn't want to be seen like that. "And whatever you want me for, the answer is no. No, thanks. Not interested. Not in anything. Nope."

Fine, choice made. Stella turned away from Beatrix and Musa and bore down on the Water Fairy Aisha like a golden ship, trusting the sea to take her to victory.

"Hello there! I'm Stella."

The girl's brown eyes widened. "Like . . . Princess Stella?"

"The very one," she confirmed. "The future queen. Not to brag! I don't want to intimidate you. Well, I don't mind intimidating you, but I'm not meant to actually say that."

The girl was staring. Had Stella gone too far? No, Stella decided, giving a light tinkling laugh to pass the moment off. She'd been frank and charming.

"I think I'm okay so far," said the girl. "I'll let you know if I find you overly intimidating in the future."

"Aisha!" Stella exclaimed. "Pretty name! Am I right in thinking you're a Water Fairy?"

Aisha's composure faltered slightly. "Yes."

"Splendid," said Stella, taking hold of her arm. "Come this way."

Aisha pulled her arm away and gave Stella an upsettingly clear-eyed glare. Could she not do Stella a favor and be dazzled by royalty?

"May I ask why?"

"Well . . ." said Stella, and thought fast. "I'm actually a mentor!"

She almost choked getting the words out, which was odd. Perhaps she was feeling a little guilty about lying to a younger girl, but it wasn't really lying. In a way, Stella was a mentor to the whole school. She was teaching them to be fabulous by example.

She avoided any further sort of fibbing by simply explaining her plan. "I'm going to show you around the school and ask you for a small demonstration of your skills."

At the mention of her skills, Aisha's gaze dropped to the ground. Ah, someone was a little self-conscious about their powers. Stella sensed victory, after all.

"You don't want to let down your mentor, do you?"

"No!" burst out Aisha. "Of course not!"

Stella said, "Excellent."

She kept to Aisha's side during the tour around the castle, watching as the group's gaze traveled over the light magic winking along the arches and wrapped like radiant vines around the pillars of the hall and the courtyard. Inwardly, Stella preened. What mattered was what people saw, her mother always said, and thanks to Stella these new kids were seeing Alfea at its best.

"What's that way?" asked Aisha.

Stella kindly shared her knowledge. "The abandoned East Wing. We don't go near it, because it's abandoned."

"Is it an unsafe structure?" asked Aisha the buzzkill Water Fairy, wrinkling her nose. "Shouldn't it be torn down if it is?"

"I heard people have parties in it," piped up the girl Beatrix behind them.

Ricki was walking beside Beatrix, conscientiously doing her part for Orientation Day and taking care of the younger fairies. At this question of Beatrix's, Ricki whistled and looked guiltily away in the direction of the old red barn doors.

Professor Harvey turned around, mild eyes inquiring behind his glasses. Professor Harvey had probably never been invited to parties, even when he was young.

Stella opened her mouth to say, *Parties, I have never heard of such a thing*, and found herself saying, "I went to one party there. I don't particularly recommend it."

Either Professor Harvey didn't hear Stella or chose not

156

to make an issue out of it. Stella closed her mouth tight to prevent any more of these weird impulses toward honesty getting her in trouble.

When the right time came, Stella grasped Aisha's arm again and dragged her around the back of the castle, to the Specialists' lake and the lawn smooth as green silk. Under Stella's careful monitorship, the grounds were strategically alight in the same way as the school. One winged statue was holding a bright scepter now, and the Specialist platforms shimmered.

Now was Stella's moment. The rest of the group was watching the Specialists train, or were being gathered up and cared for by Sky. She could trust Sky to keep people occupied. She hadn't asked him to distract anybody—Sky wasn't made for deceit—but Stella knew Sky would reliably try to scoop up lost ducklings and press guidance upon them.

If only Ms. Dowling would come. Sky had reported that Professor Harvey said she was returning today, so where was she?

Stella had left a note for Ms. Dowling on Ms. Dowling's desk, signed by Callum, and another for Callum on Callum's desk, signed by Ms. Dowling. The notes weren't explicitly romantic, but each note asked the other to meet in the maze. If Riven was right, it was tryst time. But if Stella was right . . . things would certainly be awkward for Callum.

"What if I say no to helping you?" the girl, Aisha, asked.

"Mmm, but what does 'no' mean, really?" Stella returned. "You want to show everybody what you can do, right? You want to prove that you belong here."

Aisha stared as though Stella had shone a light on her very soul rather than simply describing how Stella herself felt when she was at Alfea, and how she'd imagined someone else might feel, too.

Stella shot the other girl a smug smile. "Sounds like a yes to me."

Callum Hunter had slunk across the lawn ten minutes ago, heading for the maze with a vaguely panicked air. He hadn't seemed like a man going to a romantic tryst.

"I don't even understand why you want me to do this," Aisha continued.

"Aisha, Aisha, Aisha," said Stella. "If we're not in control of every tiny aspect of our lives, what do we have?"

"Emotional health?" Aisha suggested.

"Never heard of it," Stella told her, then frowned slightly at herself. This wasn't projecting her usual *chic* attitude.

There was Ms. Dowling at last, striding at a fast pace across the lawn and wearing a trim, fitted olive dress with deep pockets. Ms. Dowling was stylish, though in a low-key way. Stella didn't really do low-key, but she appreciated it.

Don't worry, Ms. Dowling, Stella told her silently. *I shall prove Riven's scurrilous accusations false. Then I shall make him do everything I say!*

Though every moment she felt less confident that Riven was a good enough match for Ricki.

That girl Aisha was studying Stella with suspicion. "What's going on?"

Stella stared after Ms. Dowling. "I was just thinking how impossibly confident someone must be not to desperately want everyone's eyes on her. My mother thinks that if people aren't looking at you, nothing you do counts. And what I do has to matter. I don't want to disappear into the dark."

Aisha blinked. "Excuse me?"

She was right to be confused because what Stella was saying was outrageous! Stella looked back for a moment, across the glittering waters to Sky, who might help her. That tragic floral girl Terra had talked about truthbells, Stella recalled with a prickle of unease. What if, somehow by accident, she'd taken some?

No, Stella couldn't worry about absurdities right now. She faced forward and took Aisha with her into the maze, following in Ms. Dowling's footsteps. It was time to see her plan accomplished.

MIND

Musa tried to stick to the back of the group and kept her headphones on for protection. She wasn't here to bond. She was here to see if she could stand to be trapped in a nest of other people's thoughts in exchange for learning how to tamp down her mind powers.

A couple people had asked her her name, but she regretted even telling the weird princess. Musa wasn't sharing personal information. She hadn't even decided if she wanted to come here yet.

Musa widened her eyes at all the rest of the people who asked, smiled pleasantly, and gestured to her headphones. "I can't hear you," she proclaimed.

After that, the others took the hint and left her alone to admire the school. Musa thought of herself as a postmodern type, but Alfea was okay if you liked a big historic pile of old granite. The doors on the other side of the hall were glass, with wrought iron branches and vines set against the glass in an intricate fretwork that made the castle seem surrounded by iron briars.

She drew slightly closer to the group, away from the briars, and Musa's mind brushed up against that blue-streaked girl Aisha's, getting worry and self-consciousness, all focused on her powers. Usually most people's anxiety was far more free-floating than this. Aisha seemed a purposeful girl.

Honestly, Musa was deeply jealous of people who had to concentrate to turn their magic on. Hers came as easy as breathing. Breathe in, and in came the rush of intrusive thoughts, breathe out and push them back. Pushing them back was a futile effort, since new thoughts would always rush in. All Musa could do was try to hold her breath.

Aisha's tsunami-strong wish to come to Alfea made Musa look around and appreciate it a little more, though.

Under Professor Harvey's gentle supervision, they viewed walls adorned with dozens of black-and-white photographs, and stretches of bamboo against dark green, large picture frames full of bright, living leaves and pink flowers.

Finally, they followed him into the cafeteria. There was food laid out for them on a vast table that Musa figured was several tables put together to give the appearance of a feast. It was mainly an assortment of gleaming fruit, a rainbow of colors: oranges and pears and apples and of course, other, stranger fruit as well.

"Oooh, pears," murmured someone in an overly enthusiastic voice.

Musa hated pears.

"They say watch what you eat here," murmured another girl to Musa, dark-eyed with a plaid skirt and lacy black tights. "If you eat fairy fruit, of course you have to stay. I'm Beatrix."

After some consideration, Beatrix selected a shiny red apple.

Musa pointed apologetically to her headphones. "I can't hear you."

"Mmm," said Beatrix, sinking her white teeth into the red surface. "Is that so? I just love apples."

Musa considered the fairy fruit, then considered the milling crowd: the regal blonde princess who was trying so hard to run the show, the pear enthusiast wearing a floral print, the girl with blue in her hair standing uneasily beside the blonde, the two teachers displaying very different attitudes to teaching. She took the fruit and stowed it away in her pocket. She didn't have to decide yet.

They went upstairs and along a passageway with a glass balcony rail adorned with white patterns of wings, to see dorms with diamond-paned windows and classrooms complete with glass-fronted bookshelves and mantelpieces that bore wrought iron flowers. Then they trooped back down into the hall so they could make their way out into the gardens.

Above the great hall was a domed glass ceiling, letting light pour in over the stone.

Beatrix, the girl in the plaid skirt with the tricky mind, winked at Musa. "A gust of air magic and I'm on top of the world with glass floors."

Musa gave her a small smile, but fell back another step, so she trailed the group as they were shown around the greenhouse with its marble floor and designs like jewelry around the curvilinear roof, and flowering plants dropping from the roof like veils.

"That's jasmine," the girl who liked pears and must have been an Earth Fairy contributed, addressing Beatrix with a hopeful air.

"Did not ask," Beatrix told her earnestly, and the Earth Fairy drooped like a flower that hadn't been watered.

The group went out into the sunken gardens and sculpted shrubs, the parterre, the granite forecourt, the water magic–powered clock tower, and the statues of famous fairies and eagles and phoenixes and wyverns like the ones at the foot of the grand staircase indoors. Winged things, commemorated in stone. Winged like fairies used to be, the old stories said, but that was long ago. Figured that Musa had been born centuries after the era of flying.

Beatrix gave her a speculative glance, but Musa wasn't here to make friends, and she got a weird feeling about Beatrix. Brushing by Beatrix's mind was like approaching the maze on the Alfea grounds. So many twists and turns. Safer to listen to music and look at the flowers, big drifts of yellow, blazes of color, and little spots of white like pearls in the grass.

"Those are rhododendrons," piped up the girl who was probably an Earth Fairy. "And *Rhododendron luteum*, and *Libertia grandiflora*, and shooting stars."

Musa decided to avoid the roving beseeching eye of the Earth Fairy, who hadn't been on the bus and who was trying to befriend everyone in sight. That girl wasn't a maze. That girl was ground zero for an anxiety explosion.

The Earth Fairy, who wore a flower in her hair as well as a floral blouse, gave up on catching Musa's eye and said, "I'm Terra."

"I can't hear you," murmured Musa.

She hoped that would be enough, as it had been for everyone else, and was mildly alarmed when Terra took a deep breath and shouted at the top of her lungs, "I'M TERRA!"

"Got it, you're Terra and you can't take a hint," Musa muttered, but under her breath so Terra wouldn't hear her. She didn't want to be mean. She just didn't want to be involved. She gave Terra a firmly uncomprehending smile and turned away.

A Specialist boy with blond hair who was looking sweaty and harried decided to show Beatrix and Dane around the lakes. Their faces indicated they'd been taken hostage by a very polite kidnapper.

"Please let me show you around," the blond boy told everybody. "Does anyone need directions to the restroom? My name's Sky. I live to feel useful."

Oh no, Specialist boy, what are you doing? Musa asked him silently. *Please say that in your indoor brain! Then only I will know about your problems, and I try not to listen.*

Secondhand embarrassment caused her gaze to swing wildly across the lawn. The tall blonde princess with the beauty marks and the tip-tilted nose, the one who dressed like a glittery politician, had her pastel-polished hooks firmly in Aisha and wasn't letting her escape.

"I'm not sure . . ." Aisha was mumbling.

The blonde said, in an intensely intense voice: "If people don't comply with my schemes, perhaps the whole castle will fall to ruin!"

164

If Musa had a gold coin for every stunning blonde with absolutely no filter she'd witnessed at Alfea, she'd now have two gold coins. Which wasn't that many, but it was weird it had happened twice.

Her attention was diverted from Aisha and the golden girl by the sight of what Professor Harvey said were the Specialists' lakes. There were black platforms set beside the parallel lakes and spanning over the gleaming waters. Each of the platforms was inscribed with a red slash of wings and a blue *A* for Alfea. To the side were arrows and bows and swords laid out in carved boxes, frames for doing push-ups, punching bags and boxing gloves and staffs lined up for the taking.

On one platform there was a slim girl with a cloud of dark hair pinned back, fighting a huge, hulking boy. The girl was winning, springing lightly from foot to foot and kicking the lumbering boy in the face. It made Musa think of dancing, and how much she'd loved it, and why. No minds, only bodies.

She was a Mind Fairy, not here to become one of the Specialists wandering around in their dark uniforms, sleeveless or with an undershirt of long sleeves, unadorned or with additions of leatherwork and chain mesh for armor. Their most colorful option was a khaki-colored sweater. Maybe not being a Specialist was for the best: Musa preferred her purple bomber jacket to a dark uniform. No matter what Musa wanted, her power meant she couldn't be a fighter. But it was still fun to watch. She was tempted to sink down on one of the rough benches by the platforms, under the sycamores, and watch the dark-haired girl claim her victory.

Musa didn't realize she was smiling until a different Specialist boy approached her. Her smile faded.

He was cute in a scruffy, leather-jacket, fake-smile way, Musa thought for an interested second. Then her mind took a step back from her body and said, *Hold up, girl. His mind's a mess.*

"Watching the Specialists?" he asked. "Kat wiping the floor with Mikey is a beautiful sight."

Musa's body took a step back as well. Whatever was going on under that brown hair that was trying to be curly and giving up halfway, she wanted no part of it.

"Hey, now," the boy drawled at her. "Don't get the wrong idea. I'm not trying to pester the fresh meat."

"You may be giving people the wrong impression by referring to new girls as 'fresh meat,'" said Musa.

"How heedlessly objectifying of me," said the boy, sharp for a moment and then sinking the sharp under an affected casual air. "My name's Riven."

"Sorry for you, but not my problem," Musa murmured.

"I'd like you to help me with something."

"When guys approach me, the first thing I notice is *the sheer audacity of you!*" Musa snapped. "I'm not interested in helping you with anything."

A few people turned to the sound of her raised voice. Musa deeply resented him for making her cause a scene, when Musa's only wish was to fade into the background. This Riven was trouble and she wanted no part of it.

"Hey, I'm not trying to be a creep, I just want your opinion on something!" Riven argued. "Could you come look at a couple of people and tell me whether they're romantically involved!"

Musa went still. Oh no, how had he known she was a Mind Fairy? How could he possibly have known? It wasn't the kind of thing she liked to spread around. As soon as people knew, they wanted her to read everybody's feelings but their own. Once they realized she couldn't stop reading theirs, too, they receded from her with speed. Nobody was confident enough to like having their hearts read.

Her mom used to say that one day Musa would meet people who would trust her enough that they wouldn't mind being vulnerable with her. That one day Musa would let herself be an open book to them in return.

Yeah, her mom used to say a lot of stuff. Until her mom died in agony that she kept trying to stifle so Musa wouldn't be able to feel it, too. Musa had tried to share the pain between them, but it was overwhelming. When the pain got bad enough, her mother couldn't even try to hide it from her anymore. In the end Musa drew back from her mother, terrified and hurting, unable to bear even the echo of her death throes.

That was where being close to people led. Musa didn't want to read an open book, when the story was all pain.

Musa hadn't been able to find her way back to the world since.

"Well?" prompted Riven.

"Okay!" she hissed. "I'll do it. In exchange, don't spread the word around about me, all right?"

Riven gave her a weird look. "Uh—all right? This way."

Against her better judgment, Musa followed Riven into the maze. They went past a statue of a fairy child, wingless and forlorn, clinging to a book as if desperate for knowledge.

THE HEART GROWS OLD

Vanessa Peters knew her daughter was magic. She didn't know why others couldn't see it. She was amazed Bloom didn't seem to know it herself.

Before Bloom, Vanessa's life had seemed charmed. She'd been born on a summer day in California, and it had been almost all bright California days since then. Straight As and cheerleading, becoming prom queen with a crowd of best girlfriends, followed by college and Michael Peters falling in love with her at first sight. If you stayed on course, things always worked out, that was Vanessa's philosophy. Juggling her blossoming career and a baby? She couldn't wait. Ask anyone from her cheer squad: Vanessa was flexible and determined. Falling from the top of the pyramid was something that happened to other people.

Then the doctors told her and Michael that the baby had a heart defect, that their daughter wouldn't live a day after being born. Michael held her hand and cried.

Vanessa refused to cry. She wouldn't accept what they told her was inevitable. Sometimes you wobbled and lost your balance on the pyramid, but you could regain it. She continued taking her prenatal vitamins and going to her birthing classes. She painted the nursery by herself and learned to make very bad booties, setting her teeth with every stitch she dropped.

Being driven and determined had always got her what she wanted before.

When she had the baby, Vanessa saw from the doctors' faces that her resolve hadn't produced a miracle. The doctors were going to try, as she'd tried. Everyone was trying their best, her baby's heart was trying to beat, yet it was all useless.

Until it wasn't. Until time seemed to stop, and the miracle happened.

"I've never seen anything like it in my life," said the doctor, and went on about how unprecedented it was, telling them that the baby's heart was perfect, words that Michael hung on to desperately.

Vanessa was barely able to hear the doctor at all. She was occupied staring into her baby's face, smooth as a newborn pearl. It was as though her daughter had never known a moment of pain. As if she was an entirely different child, beamed to Vanessa whole and perfect, straight from Vanessa's dreams. She gazed, enraptured, and her heart tumbled fathoms deep and was lost. For the first time in her life, Vanessa fell, helpless.

She thought everything would be perfect from then on. But desperate love didn't make everything easy. Love complicated everything, and the complications went deep as the love.

It was a golden California morning, like any other California morning, when Vanessa read that the antiques store they'd visited had caught fire. She went right upstairs to Bloom's bedroom and had to knock and wait before Bloom would answer the door.

"Come in, Mom," Bloom called after a long period of rustling and clanking, and Vanessa went in and told her daughter the news.

"Wasn't there a nasty fire in your science lab the other day?" Vanessa asked, and gave Bloom a hug. "Take care of yourself. They say things always go in threes."

"So, no juggling lit matches? Man, there go my weekend plans."

Vanessa laughed, but she wished Bloom did have weekend plans. Bloom was such a loner, and it worried Vanessa. She knew Bloom believed Vanessa wanted Bloom to be a cheerleader as she had been, but that wasn't it. She wanted Bloom encircled by friends, safe and surrounded by love, protected from all harm.

When Bloom was a baby, she was very good and well behaved. Once she could walk, that changed. She was always tumbling headfirst into trouble. But when she was small, she slept soundly every night. When she was awake, she seldom cried, and looked out at the world with bright, wondering eyes. As though she was pleased to be there.

It didn't matter if her baby slept through the night, because Vanessa never did. Every hour she would wake and tiptoe to the cradle, checking to see if the baby was breathing, with her own breathing unsteady.

When Vanessa was a little kid, her friend's Irish grandmother used to tell them stories about fairies and changelings. The stories went like this: The fairies would come take away your child, and leave a pallid ailing fairy changeling in its place, and slowly but surely the changeling child would wither away. Vanessa's own story felt like the reverse of those fairy changeling tales: suddenly being blessed, having a thriving child, with a rosy bloom of health on her cheeks, put in her arms instead of a dying one.

Vanessa called the baby *Bloom*, even though she and Michael weren't the fanciful type, and Vanessa's mother said people would think they were hippies. The name fitted Bloom somehow, as more common names could not.

Don't question the miracle, Vanessa kept telling herself. Michael had accepted the miracle without questioning, loved their child without questioning, had a bond with

Bloom that was easier than the one between Bloom and Vanessa. Perhaps there were always questions and doubts in the love between mother and daughter.

"What would you say to a mother-daughter yoga class?" Vanessa asked. "My friend Stacey says hers is great fun, and I think you'd get on with her daughter, Camilla. Stacey tells me Cami's arty."

"I turned sixteen in December, Mom. I think I'm a bit old for playdates."

A hard edge had crept into Bloom's voice. Vanessa crushed an urge to snap back, have one of the squabbles that they were having more and more frequently these days. She didn't want to fight.

"Suit yourself," she said instead, turning around toward the door.

"I wish you'd be happy with me the way I am," Bloom muttered.

Vanessa turned back. "I am happy with you. I only want—"

"Me to be a little different?" Bloom returned. "Me to fit in a little better?"

Vanessa couldn't answer, because the honest answer was *Yes*. She would be so happy if Bloom learned to fit into the world better. She always remembered how it felt to go to the playground with her daughter. Bloom was so pretty in a nice dress with her red hair brushed until it shone, and the other kids just wouldn't play with her. Vanessa's heart used to break seeing Bloom wander lonely as a fire-touched cloud, trotting around playing on the swings and jungle gym all alone.

When Bloom laughed to herself, the sound was strange and more silvery than the laughter of other children, and the tree branches would rustle and bend toward her as if to say, *Come away . . .* Bloom would climb to the top of a tree and Vanessa would wait under the branches with her heart in her throat, feeling as though Bloom might launch herself from the treetop and fly away into the sky.

She left Bloom's bedroom without responding.

Then she leaned back against the door of her adored daughter's bedroom, in the beautiful home she owned with the husband she still loved, in their safe, pretty suburb. Vanessa felt exhausted.

She'd read a thousand parenting books. She'd always been a brilliant, methodical student, able to glean knowledge and put it easily into practice. Did every parent feel like they were making it all up as they went? Did every mother have the same desperate fear for her children, and feel the same disconnect from what was so precious and should be so close?

Maybe they did. They must. It couldn't be only her.

Vanessa shook her head, pulling herself together.

It would be fine. She had to keep trying harder, that was all.

Perhaps she was a little too overprotective. Sometimes she had to crush down the impulse to take Bloom's door off its hinges so she could be always watching her.

It was simple paranoia, because Bloom had almost died when she was born, Vanessa told herself. That was long ago. There was no danger. Bloom was well.

When Bloom stood apart from the other children, swaying with the wind through the trees, or climbing down from another terrifying adventure, Vanessa would run to her and swing Bloom up off her feet. Every time she was overcome by awe and thanksgiving for her miracle. Turning in a circle with Bloom's heart beating against hers, her child safe in her arms. *Baby, my baby. Oh, my baby girl.*

It hadn't mattered then, how different Bloom might be. Vanessa had many photo albums of Bloom's childhood. Every second felt so precious, it had to be immortalized. She looked through those albums a lot recently. Vanessa wished she could find a map to return to those days, when she and Bloom were still close. No matter if it was a map of a faraway land, Vanessa would walk any strange pathway to reach Bloom again.

Vanessa still woke up every night, but she didn't get out of bed anymore. She took deep breaths, closed her eyes, and assured her racing heart that it was wrong. Her daughter wasn't in danger.

She'd meant to present the lamp she'd bought at the antiques store to Bloom, but now giving her the lamp might mean revisiting this conversation. Vanessa couldn't do that today, but she wanted Bloom to have the lamp just the same. Bloom had been terribly excited about buying it, had talked so enthusiastically about making that cracked old thing beautiful.

Vanessa went to get the lamp down from a shelf in her wardrobe and carried it back, standing outside Bloom's bedroom with it in her hands. The passageway was dark and the lamp was dark, but Vanessa knew her girl. Bloom would make it bright.

She bent and left the lamp at her daughter's door as a silent offering, to say: *I love you so much. I'm sorry we never seem to understand each other. I'd give you the world, Bloom. Then I'd give you another world, if there was one.*

Fairy Tale #5

I know that I shall meet my fate

Somewhere among the clouds above;

Those that I fight I do not hate

Those that I guard I do not love . . .

—*W. B. Yeats*

WATER

At the heart of the maze, surrounded by high beech hedges, was a stilled fountain, its waters covered by lily pads. Only a gleam could be seen here and there among the soft green.

Aisha had a bad feeling about this.

"Wait for it," murmured Stella.

Aisha wasn't certain of what the princess's plan was, exactly. Stella assured her that she had one, and that Aisha only had to play her part.

There was a man in a corduroy jacket waiting on the other side of the lily pads, wringing his hands with energetic nervousness, and a woman with a direct gaze staring at him from their side of the fountain.

There was something about the woman that made Aisha think she was important. She must be a teacher here to measure Aisha's power. Right, it made sense that there would be tests of your skill on Orientation Day. That was the way the school worked. Alfea looked for magic potential when they admitted fairies, scouring the land for fairies who could serve the realms well. But Aisha was the one who'd wanted to go to Alfea, who'd approached them asking for admittance, not the other way around. This was her chance to display the magic skills she'd worked her ass off acquiring.

"May I ask why you called me here, Callum?" the woman asked the man, skirting the fountain to his side. "I've only just arrived back, and I must attend to Orientation Day."

The man's eyes turned into perplexed saucers. "Me call *you* here?"

Princess Stella commanded, "*Now.*"

As though she was surging forward in a race, Aisha flung her power at the still waters beneath the lily pads. The fountain surged into life, a bright wave that became a great joyous splash up into the air.

Stella let go of Aisha's arm and lifted her hands. The splash rose against a backdrop of pure, brilliant light. As light magic hit the water, the water shone so brilliantly Aisha gasped and turned her head aside to escape being blinded. She felt her power slip out of her grip again. Stella's flash of power turned the whole world white.

When Aisha was able to look again, she saw the splash had become a small tornado of water, twisting silvery bright against the sky and light, then falling like a tidal . wave over the tall trees overhanging the maze, and the man and woman both. The man gave a screech of terror and catapulted himself backward into the beech hedge, leaving the woman to get the worst of the water. She went still as a statue, drenched yet somehow still dignified.

"I pictured this going very differently," Stella whispered under her breath. "I pictured soft lighting wrapping around a playful fountain of water, and droplets glistening in her hair as he gazed at her in awe!"

Aisha gazed at Stella. Not in awe.

There was the sound of dozens of running footsteps as a crowd came rushing into the maze, attracted by the crash of water, the beacon of light above the hedge, and the screams.

The first people to appear around the hedges were a Specialist boy and a girl wearing a purple bomber jacket and headphones. They both stared at the scene before them. Who could blame them? Anyone would stare.

The next to arrive were those in authority.

Specialist Headmaster Silva took one look at the situation, then strode two steps forward, wrenching off his black military jacket and throwing it at the woman. She plucked the garment out of the air without a second glance, swirling the black material and settling Silva's jacket over her shoulders. Her air of command made it suddenly very clear who she must be.

Oh no. Aisha's heart sank like a stone thrown in a pool. She had made a horrible mistake.

"Callum, go get yourself cleaned up. Stella," said Headmistress Dowling, "I'd like a word in private. After I have given the speech concluding orientation, and we have seen our guests off."

Stella hung her proud golden head.

Aisha hadn't been at Alfea much more than an hour, and she'd already lost control of her power and soaked the most important person in the whole school. Yet she wasn't someone who shirked responsibility. That was being a bad teammate.

Aisha cleared her throat and caught Headmistress Dowling's eye. "Uh, hello? I'm Aisha. I mean, I'm so sorry. I was . . . I was the one who let my water magic get out of control just then."

Ms. Dowling's gaze traveled across Aisha's face. "I don't believe using your powers was entirely your idea."

"Oh no, it wasn't!" Aisha assured her, sacrificing Stella without a qualm. "It was Stella's. She told me she was a mentor, and I wanted to prove myself. But I wasn't— Water is in my nature, but the power has never come all that naturally to me, and I know you saw the magic slip through my fingers. But I don't think it should disqualify me from attending Alfea!" she added desperately. "I can hold on to the water magic if you give me a chance. I swear."

The woman's eyes were brown as the bark of the trees behind them. Her face was severe, but it slowly dawned on Aisha, as she stared beseechingly at her, that those eyes were kind.

"You were not invited to the Orientation Day at Alfea to be tested," Ms. Dowling told her. "You were called here to be made welcome. Water magic is always a slippery power. At Alfea, you will be taught to channel it properly. As the headmistress, I must apologize to you if any of my students' behavior has made you feel you did not belong here. Let me assure you that you do."

If Aisha had expected anything after making such a

spectacular mess of the situation, it hadn't been this. The relief was so intense, it felt like a triumph in itself.

"Oh," whispered Aisha. "Oh, thank you."

"You certainly aren't in any trouble," Ms. Dowling assured her. "Allow Professor Harvey to resume showing you around the school. I shall see you at the concluding speech, and—I hope—at Alfea next year."

Professor Harvey hurried forward at Ms. Dowling's command, and Aisha retreated thankfully to his side.

Before she left the maze, Ms. Dowling said, "Aisha? One more thing."

Aisha looked back for her last glimpse of the headmistress of Alfea standing under the green trees. This lady was stern, but Aisha could get behind stern.

"You really must focus on meticulously shaping your power and making water bend to your will," warned Ms. Dowling. "Discipline is key."

Her first lesson in Alfea. She couldn't help smiling.

Aisha only just stopped herself from answering, "Yes, Coach."

MIND

Musa was accustomed to the chaos of people's minds constantly swirling about her. She wasn't used to witnessing actual catastrophe in a maze, light and water magic colliding with brilliant force. She wasn't sure what kind of mess she'd been dragged into.

One thing was extremely clear. She stood by that idiot Riven's side and ran her eyes over the dude cringing in the hedge and the lady who'd had half a fountain dumped on her. She didn't even need her powers to discern the truth, but she let the purple glow of her magic turn on them for an instant just to be 100 percent sure.

"That man and woman aren't even slightly romantically interested in each other," said Musa flatly.

"You're a Mind Fairy?" Riven sounded stunned.

Musa was stunned as well. "You didn't *know* I was a Mind Fairy?"

"Uh . . . no," said Riven.

"Then why did you ask me to come with you into a maze and assess whether two people were randomly involved? Explain yourself!"

Riven stared down at his boots. "I thought . . . woman's intuition, maybe? Also I figured it would be cool to talk to you, because you're hot?"

"I'm hot," Musa repeated. "What am I supposed to say to that?"

Riven looked up from his boots and winked. "You could say I'm hot, too."

Musa gave him the incredulous stare he deserved.

Maybe the Specialists would let her borrow a staff so she could fight him.

"Riven," said Headmaster Silva, directly behind them, his gruff voice going sinister. "Am I to understand that you had something to do with this?"

Men were so much more trouble than they were worth. Musa stared at the leaves on the beech hedge and tried to project an air of disassociation from this situation . . . and from Riven.

"Oh yes, this is a hundred percent my fault. And Stella's," Riven reported instantly.

The blonde princess cast a murderous glance over her shoulder. "That's absolutely true."

Both of them were shocked by their own radical honesty, Musa could see.

Ms. Dowling folded her hands in front of her, and Musa felt the surge as Alfea's headmistress summoned patience.

"Well, I'm glad you're both having enough of a crisis of conscience to confess."

"I'm not having a crisis of conscience!" protested Riven. "I barely have a conscience!"

Nobody seemed impressed by this truthfulness.

"Tell me why you did this," Silva spat.

Riven rubbed his forehead. "Uh, okay. Well, Stella was trying to set me up with her friend Ricki—"

"*What?*" said a pretty girl who Musa presumed was

Ricki, peering over Professor Harvey's shoulder with her eyes and mouth gone wide. Musa felt she could sympathize with Ricki's shocked dismay.

"Shut up, Riven!" Stella snarled. "I'm so sorry, Ricki. I see now it was a terrible mistake!"

"Sure, that was never going anywhere, because it's obvious who Ricki actually likes," Riven continued.

"Shut up, Riven!" Ricki's voice went high with panic.

Musa sent out a questing tendril of power due to vague curiosity, but then as her mind brushed Ricki's, she got a taste of genuine terror that crushed her curiosity down. Who Ricki actually liked was none of Musa's business.

"Why's it always 'Shut up, Riven!' and never 'Keep talking, Riven, you're doing great'?" Riven wanted to know.

"Keep talking, Riven, you may be expelled or killed," encouraged Headmaster Silva. "I haven't decided yet."

Riven seemed understandably stressed by this declaration. "Okay, so we had a theory about Headmistress Dowling's love life—"

Headmaster Silva's outraged protectiveness toward Headmistress Dowling was as obvious to Musa as Silva's coat hurled through the air so Dowling would catch it.

"Shut up," ordered Silva. "Right now."

"Isn't that slightly contradictory . . ." began Riven.

Silva rounded on Riven as though there was a weapon in his hand, or soon would be. "I see you have chosen death."

Riven went quiet. It was a good look on him, Musa thought. He should keep it up.

The taller Specialist boy, who was blond and meant well, came over and asked Musa quietly, "Is he bothering you?"

"Am I bothering her?" Riven scoffed. "I'm not the one who was forcing directions on literally every new face he saw, Sky."

"I'm just trying to help—" began Sky, and bit his lip.

He and Riven both beamed out distress in every direction for any innocent Mind Fairy to be assailed with. Musa was getting such a headache from this mess. Contrary to expectations, peace seemed in short supply at Alfea. Maybe this school wasn't for her.

"He *is* bothering me," Musa reported.

"I'll take him away," volunteered Sky.

"I can take myself away!" snapped Riven, and did so, storming off into the maze.

He was going the wrong way and would inevitably get stuck in the maze. Musa and Sky exchanged a glance, confirming they both knew this, and watched him go.

Unexpectedly, Stella was the one who went after him. Musa saw Stella catch up to Riven just before he turned the corner into the passageways of the maze. Riven seemed extremely startled to see her.

"You lost our bet, Riven." Stella gave him a terrifyingly bright smile that made Musa wonder if she used light magic on her teeth. "And there's no chance Ricki will date you now."

"There was never any chance," grumbled Riven.

"Which means that you are of no further use to me!" declared Stella. "Except that I'm in a very bad mood, and your humiliation might cheer me up. Now listen . . ."

She took hold of his elbow and dragged him away to his doom. They both disappeared into the maze.

"Sorry about Riven," the boy called Sky told Musa.

"Yep, if he were my friend I'd be sorry, too," said Musa.

Sky blinked, radiating distress again. *Stop this*, Musa willed him. *Why must boys have so many feelings?*

"I hope whatever Riven did hasn't affected the way you think about Alfea. I know he doesn't make the best first impression, but this is a great school. I mean it."

The crowd was receding out of the maze now, the dramatic scene played out. Musa walked slowly out by Sky's side. He was staring at her, his desire to make up for his friend burning in his mind, but Musa didn't actually require directions.

"Your friend won't be a factor in my final decision. I wasn't sure about Alfea before I met him. I wasn't sure about Alfea before I ever came here," Musa told him slowly. "Why did you want to go to Alfea?"

The Specialist boy called Sky blinked, as though he hadn't ever asked himself that question before. Then his dark blue eyes cleared, the color of the sea after a storm had passed.

He answered steadily, "At Alfea, they teach you to be a hero."

"I don't believe in heroes," said Musa.

"If you knew Headmaster Silva, you would," Sky told her confidently.

Musa gave him a tiny shake of the head and a tinier smile as they emerged from the maze and parted ways. Musa went off alone, the way she liked it.

She felt a little sorry for Sky. Sky's friend Riven had a mind that was a disaster waiting to happen. From all she had seen of Headmaster Silva's mind, there was a lot more guilt and anger in him than heroism. Musa didn't know if she'd ever witnessed anyone feeling heroic. Maybe there were no heroes.

Sky would realize the truth one day.

Everybody got disillusioned sooner or later.

EARTH

Terra was feeling extremely disillusioned about orientation. None of the other girls wanted to be her friend. It was just like always, except worse, because this time Terra was supposed to belong. This time the problem wasn't that Terra was too young. The problem was that Terra was *Terra*.

That girl in the purple with the headphones had looked all cool and aloof, but Terra had told herself maybe she was shy, and would appreciate Terra making an effort. That hadn't been the case.

Then there was Stella staging a weird light show for some reason, and apparently Riven wanted to date Ricki? That made sense, Terra supposed. He would date Ricki and never come to the greenhouse anymore, because he'd have better things to do. Ricki was part of Stella's set, one of the pretty, popular girls. Ricki was the kind of girl that all guys wanted, and all the girls wanted to befriend.

Terra was trying so hard to make friends! She didn't understand what she was doing wrong. She was so miserable.

Terra felt too disconsolate to join the final lap of the tour around a school she'd lived in her whole life. She'd make it back in time for Ms. Dowling's closing address, but she needed to be alone by herself for a little while, rather than alone in a crowd.

Terra stood under the trees, green and lacy with springtime, watching their reflection dance in the mirror of the sky. In the still water, she saw a flash of black and gray— the Specialists' uniform. Perhaps Riven had seen she was all by herself, and he'd come to keep her company.

190

This was a day of disappointments, though. It was a total stranger. He loomed over Terra, almost twice her size.

"Saw you lingering down here," said the guy. "Couldn't help seeing you, actually. You're not exactly wasting away, little fairy."

He winked as he spoke, as if to say he didn't mean it, but there was a glint in his eye that said he did. Mean jokes always flustered Terra. She opened her mouth, trying to think of something witty to say, and just ended up opening and closing her mouth like a fish who was bad at repartee.

"Looking for somebody? Maybe it's just anybody in uniform. Hot for Specialists, are we?" The guy winked at her.

"I beg your pardon?" said Terra.

"Do you wanna have a good time?" asked this beefy Specialist guy Terra didn't know, reaching out as if to grab her arm.

"Goodness no!" exclaimed Terra, thoroughly dismayed. This must be creepy Matt, whom her brother had warned her about.

She made a sharp gesture, calling earth magic to her, and the branches of the chestnut trees by the lake reached down and smacked Matt several times in the face. Then the grass tangled at his feet, tripping him up so he fell in the lake. Once he was in there, Terra silently asked the weeds in the lake to dunk him vigorously a few times.

"You shouldn't grab strangers. That is so rude," Terra informed him earnestly.

The Specialist burbled and choked up water as he surfaced, and she took that as an agreement he was filled with regret and would change his ways. She told the weeds to let him up after a few minutes, and then followed the path toward the greenhouse, away from the splashing and the inappropriate language.

Possibly her reaction had been disproportionate. Terra felt slightly guilty as she walked off.

No, she'd done the right thing. What if he'd alarmed one of the girls here for Orientation Day? That would make a terrible first impression of their wonderful school! Strict discipline had been called for.

She just needed to regroup, she told herself. Terra would take a teeny, tiny peek into the greenhouse, maybe put her face in the jasmine and breathe in deep. Then she'd go back out to that crowd of people who wanted nothing to do with her.

When she opened the greenhouse door and sidled in, she saw Riven standing on the diagonal line of a marble tile, in a pool of light stained green by the windowpane.

Riven brightened when he saw her. "I was hoping you'd come. This has been a terrible day, Ter. You will not believe what Stella's making me do next."

Usually, Terra would have asked with eager sympathy about what Stella was planning to do to poor Riven.

Usually, Riven and Terra didn't see each other unless

they were in the greenhouse. But they'd seen each other today. Or rather, she'd seen him, and he'd avoided her eye.

Terra just said, "Oh."

He wandered over to her. "I hate this school, Ter."

Usually, Terra would comfort Riven and say it wasn't so bad, all the while nursing a shining private vision of how great it would be to go to Alfea one day. Today, she didn't feel like comforting Riven. She wanted some comfort herself.

She wasn't getting it from Riven, that much was clear. She'd thought of them as friends, and Terra wasn't very accustomed to friendship, but she did know it wasn't supposed to go all one way.

Riven had talked publicly to that girl in purple, because she was cool and pretty. He wasn't hiding the fact he knew Terra because Terra was younger. It was because Terra was a nerd and terminally uncool. She didn't look right or act right, and Riven was embarrassed to know her. He didn't want anyone to find out that he was interested in plants, or that he hid out in the greenhouse. He'd never willingly tell another soul that he hung out with Terra while he was there, or show anybody all the stuff she'd taught him. Terra was an embarrassment. Riven was ashamed to know her.

"You hate everything, Riven," she said, more sharply than she'd ever spoken to him before. "What's so bad about Alfea?"

She saw the way her sharp tone stung his pride. But she felt she'd catered to Riven's pride plenty.

"It's a factory designed to turn us all out in little boxes," Riven answered promptly, voice gone hard. "Earth Fairy, Air Fairy, Fire Fairy, Water Fairy, Specialist, and you're never meant to be anything more or less than that. They're even crushing out Sky's individuality, and Sky barely has any."

At least Sky had been trying to help out the younger students, even if he could get slightly patriarchal I-know-everything-including-directions about it. At least Sky was trying to be good to other people. Terra was starting to think she'd got everything wrong about how Sky and Riven interacted.

She stared up at Riven with new, clear eyes, and watched his expression distort under her gaze.

"That's mean," Terra murmured, distressed.

"I am mean!" said Riven. "How have you not spotted that yet? What kind of an idiot are you?"

She stumbled back, away from him. She thought regret might have touched Riven's face for an instant, but it was chased off by anger twice as strong as any regret.

"Sorry, I was wrong," Terra told him unsteadily.

"Terra—" he began.

Terra wouldn't let herself cry. "You didn't even talk to me today. You don't want anyone to know we've ever spoken."

"No, I don't."

Riven's face had gone pale and strained, but the answer came out at once. Terra drew in a hurt breath, feeling as though she'd had her hand caught by a thorn, and made herself nod. She could handle the pain. She was the one who'd touched briars in the first place.

"You think I'm a tragic, lonely nerd who doesn't know any better than to be nice to you."

The answer came through locked teeth, but just as fast as last time. "Yeah," Riven said. "I do."

"I'm so stupid. I believed the best of you," Terra continued, numb. "Because I thought we were friends."

"I don't *want* to be your friend," snarled Riven, then bit his lip viciously hard.

Riven talked a lot, eager to come out with something clever. She'd never seen him try *not* to talk before.

Maybe he was trying not to say anything else horrible, but he'd already said enough. And what he said was obvious, anyway, to anyone who wasn't as big a fool as Terra. They'd never been friends. The greenhouse was just a convenient place for a lonely nerd to go and be bitter into a convenient ear about how much cooler he felt he should be.

"Fine," Terra told him in a clipped voice. "I completely understand. Don't you have to go be with the popular kids, Riven? Go do whatever it is Stella dared you to do. Go be a second-rate Sky."

"At least other people talk to me," Riven spat. "You think next year is going to change everything, Terra? Wait and see. You'll hate Alfea then, too."

He spun around and stormed out, banging the door behind him so hard that the panes shivered like emeralds and diamonds hanging in a necklace.

Terra braced herself against a lab table and willed herself not to cry or smash anything. Her hurt feelings didn't count. There was a problem that had to be addressed, a mess that had to be cleared up, and only Terra could do it. The way Riven had talked wasn't at all like him. He was all showy half-truths and bragging and jokes to deflect reality. He hadn't wanted to tell the truth, and he'd done it, anyway.

Someone must have fed Riven truth potion, Terra realized. Who? Stella?

"Who" didn't matter, Terra told herself. For a minute she was tempted to let Riven rot. He could go on running his mouth off to everyone and ruining his life, for all she cared. But that wasn't right. This problem had come from the greenhouse, and she should fix it. She had the tools and the knowledge, so that made this situation her responsibility. If you could do something, then you should do it.

Terra brushed away the tears at the corners of her eyes with the back of her hand and reached for the chest of silvery vials. She had to be practical. She was lonely and miserable, but she had a job to do.

WATER

There were two great stone steps in front of the doors inscribed by twisting iron branches. As the sun sank lower, the glass dome of the ceiling showed that the dome of the sky had gone from deep to silvery blue. Ms. Dowling stood at the top of the steps and addressed the future students of Alfea, with natural light turning the doors behind her into a scenic backdrop of silver trees and shadow.

"Students and future students of Alfea," said Ms. Dowling in a voice that echoed against the stone. "Thank you for being here to experience our orientation. This school was set up to help you achieve your goals and shape yourselves into the people you wish to become. I thank you for placing your faith in us. Without you, Alfea would be an empty castle in the woods. With you, Alfea is a dream that will live on."

Aisha sighed, listening raptly. Beside her, Beatrix of the plaid skirt and the notebook gave a yawn. Aisha shot her a glare.

"Show some respect, okay? I think Ms. Dowling's really inspiring."

Beatrix gave a dainty shrug. "If you believe all that." She gestured to the pillars wrapped in light and the domed glass ceiling, where the light magic was reflecting to make stars in a blue sky.

"As a token of my appreciation for your coming, we have prepared potions for luck in our greenhouse that all the fairies may collect. And I believe a Specialist is bringing forth a selection of daggers that our future Specialists may take home with . . . them . . ."

Through the silver-tree doors walked that Specialist boy Riven with an open case full of daggers, their blades shaped into steel-leaf shapes. And without his shirt. Aisha rolled her eyes.

Riven carried the case silently and laid it on the steps where Ms. Dowling stood, under the gaze of a stunned audience.

Ms. Dowling rubbed her forehead, as if to ease a violent headache. "Really, Riven?"

"Stella made me," squealed Riven. "We had a bet!"

"I'll kill him, Farah," promised Headmaster Silva, lunging forward from the shadows where he'd been standing with Professor Harvey.

Ms. Dowling hissed, "That's inappropriate!"

Silva nodded. "Right. Sorry. I'll kill him, Headmistress Dowling. I'll have him stuffed and put at the entryway of the Specialists' Hall as a terrible warning to others."

"I always suspected you were trying to kill me!" Riven exclaimed.

Silva rolled his eyes. "Don't tempt me." He lifted a hand, clearly to grab Riven by the collar, then realized Riven wasn't wearing one. With the sigh of a martyr annoyed to death, Silva grabbed Riven's ear and started to drag him out.

Ms. Dowling sighed, and asked the front row to come up and take potions and daggers. The rest of the audience broke up into gossiping chaos.

Aisha gazed around at her fellow Orientation Day attendees to share her incredulity at the turn things had taken. She caught a look of disbelief on that boy Dane's face, but it appeared to be a very different kind of disbelief to the emotion Aisha was currently experiencing. He had his eyes trained on Headmaster Silva and Riven.

"Wow, who is that?" Dane breathed.

"Yikes, he's some skinny white boy who barely has abs; get ahold of yourself," advised Aisha. "And he's showing them in a super inappropriate setting, I might add, so he's a lunatic and his abs are not worth your time. Lots of people have abs. *I* have abs, not that I'll be showing them off on this occasion. No big deal."

Dane probably had better abs himself, being very solidly built even if he wasn't that tall. But Aisha supposed whatever he was into.

"What do you mean— I wasn't looking at—" snapped Dane.

Contrary to his words, Dane was still looking. In an extremely focused fashion. Beatrix leaned forward, joining Dane's watch. Riven's admiring audience was growing.

Some people couldn't resist rule breakers, Aisha guessed. They never seemed to think maybe rules were there for a reason.

"I agree, the abs aren't bad," drawled Beatrix, and Dane gave an appreciative glance to her intricately coiled crimson-tinted braids and wicked dark eyes, before his attention went back to Riven like a compass swinging true north. "But I have more important things to think of."

Aisha gave up on the still-staring Dane as a lost cause, and turned toward Beatrix the Cynical Notebook Girl. At least she was goal oriented. Maybe they could get along, after all.

"Don't we all," agreed Aisha. "I spent the whole day trying to work out every place I can manage to swim on the grounds. My name's Aisha."

"I'm not very sporty," confessed the girl. "I plan to be very focused on my studies."

They shook hands, but Aisha regretted introducing herself. Beatrix had a slightly disdainful air about her, and her eyes were keen and unkind. Aisha felt like Beatrix could see Aisha's shortcomings with magic, and she wasn't going to be sympathetic.

"Are you looking forward to going to Alfea?" Aisha asked.

"Let's say I'm considering my options," drawled Beatrix. "Thought I'd come get the lay of the land."

Nice. Beatrix wasn't even sure if she wanted to attend Alfea, and here was Aisha desperate to go. She gave Beatrix a meaningless smile and made a vague gesture, as if she had somewhere important to be. She wandered outside and saw Beatrix whispering to the boy called Dane. Those two would probably make better friends with each other than with her.

Dispirited, Aisha trailed out of the castle and down the steps to the sunken garden, and almost tripped over the girl with headphones crouching behind a carefully clipped tree.

"Oh," Aisha said, startled. "Hey—I don't know your name. Are you okay?"

"I'm Musa. And I'm just a little overwhelmed," admitted Musa, and shook her head, her hoop earrings swaying. "It's been—so much, all day."

Aisha's own earrings were hoops, too, but far smaller, and with a turquoise dangling from each. She wasn't sure she could pull off Musa's huge hoops, or her punk-rock-Princess-Leia hairdo, but both worked on Musa.

"Sorry to disturb you," she said. "I'll go."

Musa shook her head again. "It's okay."

It had been Aisha's intention to go down and look at the Specialists' lakes. It was soothing for her to gaze at water and center herself before she had to climb back on the bus. If she could have, she would've taken a quick dip and seen how long it took her to do ten laps in one of those lakes.

But Musa had said it was okay to stick around, and actually Aisha felt that Musa shouldn't be alone. Musa looked really shaky, folded up in on herself as if under a massive burden Aisha couldn't see. The least Aisha could do was stay.

So Aisha stayed, keeping silent watch by the tree, as Musa listened to music until her breathing was a little more steady and she looked a little less like she might crumble away if she had to bear another second's interaction with a person.

"I like your earrings," Aisha offered at last.

Musa's teeth gleamed in a small smile. "I like your hair."

That tribute from a stylish girl made Aisha feel more optimistic about her hair. She did love the color. She could just fix up the blue in it, so they were proper streaks instead of patches. Then, Aisha thought with gathering confidence, she'd look great.

"I was overwhelmed when we came to Alfea, too," Aisha admitted. "But then I thought, 'Hey, maybe Alfea's going to be fun.'"

"Maybe," said Musa. "Thanks for being chill."

"What can I say? Water Fairy. We're always chill."

Aisha made a little gesture that caused dewdrops to skip along the air, like skipping a pebble across the water. She and Musa watched the sparkling arc together, like a tiny crystal rainbow that streamed out into the mountains on the horizon, and Aisha smiled in victory.

For once, the magic had worked perfectly.

SPECIALIST

Just because it was Orientation Day and everyone he knew was acting deranged didn't mean Sky got to skip his sunset run around Alfea. He ran under the branches of the trees and the gathering shadows, and repressed a startled yell when Terra popped up in his path like a mushroom.

"I owe you an apology," exclaimed Terra. "For many things. Many, many . . ."

Terra's voice sank into a trouble burble, containing the words *Riven* and *bullied*.

"Is Riven in some kind of trouble?" Sky asked. "You'd better tell me if he is." He paused. "Wait, is this about me going hard on him when we're training? I do that to help him get better! He has a lot of potential."

He didn't understand why this was apparently so hard for people to understand. Terra's eyes were gleaming with what appeared to be remorseful tears.

Maybe Terra had seen the Specialists sparring and jumped to some wrong conclusions? It was true fairies didn't fight as Specialists did. Silva had always warned Sky to be careful around Sam, adding "if he's anything like Ben."

That probably applied to Terra as well. "I'm sorry you were upset," Sky told Terra carefully.

"Of course, you weren't bullying him!" Terra exclaimed. "I see it all now. You were just trying to help him. We

203

should both be grateful to you, but he's an ungrateful, evil weasel—"

"Steady on, Terra."

Sky was familiar with highly strung people, but Terra was literally vibrating.

"I'm sorry I ever doubted you," Terra told him earnestly. "Especially if it hurt your feelings."

"It didn't because I didn't know you . . . did doubt me," said Sky.

"You are a great guy and a wonderful person!"

"Thank . . . you . . ." said Sky.

"I'm sorry about all the vines I set to trip you and also the bush of sword-length thorns I grew to trap you."

Sky blinked. "I'm sorry, the *what*?"

Terra frowned and then started nodding rapidly. "I guess you haven't come across the thornbush yet. Yeah, that's probably for the best. I'll handle it. Forget I said anything!"

He thought that a bush full of sword-length thorns would be hard to forget, actually. But Terra was blinking up at him, and she looked small with sorrow, like the little girl playing with her brother in the gardens of Alfea when Sky trotted by with Silva and a sword. He'd never learned how to talk to her, and he didn't think he could start now, but he didn't want her to be sad. Besides, the girl grew sword-length thorns at the drop of a hat, it seemed best for her to stay calm.

Sky smiled and nodded. "Okay, I will."

"Also, you've been poisoned," continued Terra.

Terra was poisoning people now? Why was that? That was an alarming thing for her to be doing. People said Stella was scary, but Stella didn't poison people and she had far more social graces than Terra.

Compared to being poisoned, Stella was very restful.

Sky mumbled, "I feel fine, though . . ."

"I'm pretty sure from all the things you were saying today that you were given a truth potion," Terra explained. "But! I can fix it. I made the antidote. And two more in case . . . anybody else needs it. I think one person might? Not sure who, and I don't care, either! And you should have a spare."

Under the meandering flow of Terra's one-person conversation Sky remembered, with an uneasy lurching feeling, what he'd said to Silva that morning. That hadn't been like him at all.

She offered him three small vials of liquid, glittering fierce dark blue in the sunset. They were stoppered up with wax seals that had pansies printed on the top. It was odd that Terra had carefully packaged the antidote, but she was an odd girl. She did wear a lot of flower-patterned clothes.

He still didn't know why she'd poisoned him, but now she was looking at him with an intent and imploring gaze. He supposed it wasn't Terra's fault that he had made a fool of himself in front of Silva. A truth potion was a good thing, because telling the truth was good. It was Sky's own fault that he'd messed up.

"Don't worry, Terra," he told her gently.

Sky took the vials, putting two into his jacket. He unstoppered the last one and poured the blue liquid directly into his mouth.

Terra ran at Sky and hugged him. They didn't know each other well enough for this, but Sky patted her gingerly on the back regardless.

She beamed up at him, eyes glittering in the setting sun. "I'd totally tell a friend you were one of the rare true good guys out there. If I had any friends. And if you weren't dating Stella. Haha. I want to live."

She disengaged, gave Sky a thumbs-up, and scampered off. Sky stared after her. That had been an intensely strange interaction.

Then he resumed his run around the castle.

He had barely begun the race when he heard a girl scream.

LIGHT

Ms. Dowling had told Stella to meet her in her office.

Stella entered with her heart beating hard, full of dread—she was in trouble, she'd be punished—and was surprised when the sight of the headmistress in her office calmed her heartbeat instead of sending it racing.

Ms. Dowling wasn't a vision on a throne. She stood by her desk, flanked by her old books and her globe of the fairy realms, and she looked stern but also calm and reasonable. She might punish Stella, but she wouldn't hurt her.

Ms. Dowling had dried off and changed before giving her closing speech. She was wearing a rust-brown dress now rather than an olive-green one. Her hair was piled up on her head, dark-gold tendrils falling. There was a gold medallion with a symbol that could be the Tree of Knowledge on it around her neck, and no other jewelry. When she saw Stella, Ms. Dowling gave her a smile, even though Stella was in trouble. It wasn't a dazzling smile. Ms. Dowling's mouth barely moved, but her face was touched with humor just the same.

Everybody said Queen Luna was the most beautiful woman in all the realms, more beautiful than Stella could ever be, but Stella liked looking at Ms. Dowling's face more.

"Matters got slightly out of hand today, didn't they, Stella?" Ms. Dowling asked.

"Don't be disappointed in me and don't be angry with me!" Stella burst out, then gnawed disgracefully on her lower lip, and remembered once more Terra talking about truthbells.

Even if someone had dosed her with truth potion, Stella couldn't let Ms. Dowling find out about it. She'd already disappointed her headmistress enough today. She should be able to handle this herself.

"I'm neither disappointed nor angry with you," said Ms. Dowling in her measured tones. "Well. Some irritation did occur when half a fountain was dumped on my head."

Stella winced.

"Speculating on teachers' love lives isn't particularly appropriate behavior."

"Not befitting a princess," Stella said dully.

"Not befitting any student of Alfea," Ms. Dowling corrected her. "I don't hold you to standards higher than the others. That wouldn't be fair."

Life wasn't fair. Was it fair that Stella got to be a princess, and hotter with better posture than almost anybody else? You had to pay for your privileges somehow.

"It was Riven's ridiculous idea," Stella said, and even to herself it sounded as though she was whining. Whining annoyed her mother more than anything else. Stella would be left alone in the dark longer for that.

"Riven will be disciplined appropriately by Headmaster Silva," said Ms. Dowling. "Riven is his responsibility. You are mine."

"I don't want to be a burden or a disappointment," said Stella, who hated truth potions and herself.

She focused on the glass jars lined up along Ms. Dowling's desk, not daring to meet the headmistress's eyes and see her judgment.

"You are neither," Ms. Dowling assured her. "You are a privilege."

That was a nice idea—the notion of being something lovely, like a tiara or a title, something people were proud of and wanted to live up to. Stella lifted her eyes from the jars and smiled faintly.

"Still, I would be remiss not to discipline you for misleading a future student at Orientation Day," said Ms. Dowling. "You told a Water Fairy you were a mentor? The punishment for that seems clear. Next year, if I have a student I believe may face particular difficulties, I will assign you as her mentor. Try to do better for her than you did for Aisha today."

Her mother's voice in Stella's head spat furiously that Ms. Dowling had no right to discipline a princess. Stella didn't let those words escape her lips. As relief and resentment warred within her, she only dared nod her head.

Ms. Dowling inclined hers in return. "Very good, Stella. One more thing. Today when you and Aisha combined your magic, I noticed your light magic was at an extremely high intensity. I've noted that often in class, but even more so outside class. How much are you using your light magic in day-to-day life? I fear you may be overly dependent on it."

"Don't we all depend on our magic?" Stella asked. "This is a school for learning magic!"

There was a pause in which Stella tried to be quiet and her headmistress looked thoughtful. There were circles of blue, green, and yellow around Ms. Dowling's head like giant jewels on a crown.

"That's true," said Ms. Dowling. "But your lessons do not teach that you should seize power at all costs. You're an extremely powerful fairy, Stella. But power uncontrolled can be as harmful to your friends as your enemies. Calibration is even more important than brilliance."

She wasn't speaking as though Stella was in trouble. She was speaking as though Stella was in class. The soothing cadences of education made it seem for a moment as if Stella were sitting beside Ricki at a desk in a room papered with green damask, looking out the bay windows, at peace as Ms. Dowling spoke to them in her kind, wry voice.

When Stella was queen, she wanted to make the people in her care feel like this.

"What would you say to some private lessons in calibration?" Ms. Dowling urged, and Stella was so tempted. "If you could learn to dim your magic by degrees, I think you would find you have far more control of it."

With awful clarity, Stella could imagine her mother's reaction to hearing that Stella had learned to dim her light magic. When Queen Luna always believed Stella didn't burn bright enough. And if Queen Luna learned that Stella had to have special classes because her control wasn't good enough? Her mother would think she was a failure on every level.

Stella couldn't let it happen. "I don't want to! I don't want to ask anyone for help. I didn't mean for everything to get messed up. I can do better. I will try harder. Please believe in me," Stella begged.

"Stella, I do," Ms. Dowling told her steadily. "But it is no weakness to ask for help." She forestalled Stella's protest with a single uplifted hand. "Don't be afraid."

I'm not frightened of anything, Stella wanted to scream, but she couldn't say it because it was such a lie.

"I won't force you to do anything you don't wish to. I am not saying that you need help. What I am saying is, if the time ever comes when you wish for help, you can come to me." Ms. Dowling gave an infinitesimal shrug. "That's all. You may go."

Stella found herself limp, shocked more than anything else by the unexpected reprieve. Queen Luna wasn't big on mercy. Before Ms. Dowling could change her mind, though, Stella should leave.

She scrambled up, graceless for a moment in her high-heeled boots. She almost knocked over the glass jars on Ms. Dowling's desk. Then she recovered her poise in time to make a regal exit.

"Stella?" Ms. Dowling added when Stella was at the door, head held high. "The light decorations for Orientation Day were beautiful. I loved seeing Alfea through your eyes."

"Thank you," Stella whispered.

It was terribly nice to be appreciated. She went back to her suite in a wonderful mood.

So she had to mentor some brat next year? That was no real punishment. She had sailed through this whole business with royal aplomb. And if someone had slipped

211

her truthbells as some sort of prank—Stella personally suspected Riven—she could deal with that, too. She had a suite full of best girlfriends who were also her loyal acolytes. What could go wrong?

When she got to the suite, she found Ilaria posing in the common room in front of a mirror suspended in midair, the two other girls on the sofa, and Ricki in the armchair.

"Does my ass look big in this?" asked Ilaria.

"Don't ask whether your ass looks big, ask whether your taste seems superior," advised Stella. "And frankly, it doesn't."

All right, Stella needed an antidote now. They were always holding impromptu fashion shows in the suite, and reckless fashion honesty could lead to bloodshed. Ilaria's eyes were already narrowed.

"Wait. I didn't want to admit it, because I hate admitting any weakness"—Stella hated the words coming out of her mouth and hated her own mouth for saying them—"but I need help. I think I must have been dosed with truth potion. Somebody get Professor Harvey to come cure me."

Ricki nodded at once, springing out of her armchair and making for the door, but another of Stella's suitemates barred the way. Stella remembered how they'd barred the doors so Sky couldn't come in once. It didn't seem so funny now.

Ilaria's eyes were still narrowed. Stella's stomach lurched.

Stella was more afraid of illusions than anything else,

and for a moment it seemed as though she'd been living in one. She'd believed she was surrounded by friends in Alfea.

She'd been deluded.

"Not so fast," said Ilaria, stepping up to Stella and taking a firm grasp on her arm. "While we have you here, maybe it's time for some palace gossip. You're always so close-mouthed, Princess Stella. Do you think royal secrets aren't fit for peasant ears? Tell us what it's really like to live with Queen Luna."

Not that. Anything but that.

The dancing daub of multifaceted light magic on the wall that Stella had following her around, a convenient spotlight for all occasions, burst into the destructive brightness of an exploding star. Ilaria shied away, hand slipping from Stella's arm, and Stella broke like a hunted deer from the undergrowth. The way out was barred, so she sprinted for her bedroom, only thinking about escape, a child who wanted to hide under the bedclothes.

Ilaria and the others followed her, crowding in through her door.

"It's not that serious," Ilaria said, her laugh like knives lacerating Stella's mind. "We're just curious. If we were really her friends, she'd talk to us without a truth potion. Stella, tell us just one thing—"

Stella got her back to the wall, cowering in a corner, a scared child and not a princess at all. She covered her ears, not wanting to hear their questions, biting her lip so hard her mouth filled with blood.

"Shut up, Ilaria!" Ricki said fiercely. "All of you shut up, get out, get out—"

Light filled the room, sharp-edged as though reflecting off a broken mirror. Screams broke from the other girls as they covered their eyes and cowered from the light in terror.

"Fine, Stella, have it your way like you always do!" Ilaria shouted, retreating. "Come on, Ricki, she's a psycho."

Ricki ran, but not to the door to join the others. She ran somewhere else.

"Sky!" Ricki screamed out the tower window. "Sky, come quickly, Stella needs help!"

There was a silence. Surely, Sky wasn't there. If Sky was there, he would call out a question. Stella waited, trembling, straining to hear his voice.

Instead she heard a scrape, of daggers and boots on stone. Ricki stood back from the window, and Stella wondered for a confused moment why on earth she was doing that. Then Sky came in through the window, ducking his golden head so he wouldn't hit it on the stone, and Stella realized, dazed, what had happened.

Her golden boy had climbed the tower, to rescue the princess. Stella slid to the ground, put her head in her hands, and burst into tears.

"Oh, thank you for being there, thank you, I just think you're the greatest . . ." Ricki was saying.

"It's nothing. I always run a circuit around Alfea at sunset," Sky returned absently, moving past Ricki, a man on a mission. "Stella? Oh, Stel . . ."

He dropped to his knees on the cold stone floor and gathered her into his arms. The weapon-callused hands that stroked her gold-ribboned braid were gentle.

"She said she'd been fed a truth potion," Ricki told Sky.

Sky's hand in Stella's hair stayed steady, calming. "It's all right. I have the antidote."

He took a blue vial out of his jacket. She wouldn't have taken a strange potion from anyone's hand but Sky's, but she had faith in him. It made perfect sense to her, that he would have the solution to her problems, the remedy for all her troubles. This was the boy she'd always trusted, the only one who knew her. The boy who had looked right past the queen with his steady blue eyes, and seen Stella.

"Sky." Stella's voice broke on a sob. "I don't want to be alone."

"Stel, I'm here," murmured Sky, rocking her as if she was still a child. "I'm here, I'll always be here."

She crawled into his lap, and held on to his jacket tight with both fists, and believed him. While he was there, she was protected.

So Stella would never let him go.

SPECIALIST

It took Riven a long time to explain his crimes to Headmaster Silva. Partly because by this point, he'd committed many crimes. Partly because Silva kept interrupting to yell at him.

"You thought Ms. Dowling was what? With that—her human assistant?" Silva demanded. "And you speculated about her personal life with other students and put her in an embarrassing position? Twenty laps around Alfea, now!"

Twenty laps was so many laps.

"I know Callum's kind of weaselly, but some people are into that," Riven said desperately. "And ladies have needs."

Silva's face was a steel mask. "Thirty laps. Never speak of Ms. Dowling with disrespect again."

Thirty laps was even more.

"Sorry if Ms. Dowling's your secret girlfriend, sir!" Riven exclaimed. "I didn't know! Congratulations and everything, she's hot for an old person."

The look Silva gave Riven was super distressing. *This is it*, Riven thought. *This is how I die*. Nobody would even miss him, because he'd managed to piss off everyone he knew.

"You know what, Riven?" Silva snarled. "Just keep running. I'll tell you when to stop."

"What if I don't run?" Riven suggested desperately. "I mean, can you make me?"

Silva took a single step toward him. Riven ran.

Many hours later, Riven crawled over the threshold of the Specialists' Hall. He was dying. He needed his bed. He needed water. He wondered if Sky would bring him some water while he was in bed, since he was dying.

Then he remembered he'd alienated Sky even more thoroughly than he'd alienated Terra. He dragged in a deep, weary breath and then yelped as he almost walked right into Matt.

And Matt had a black eye.

"Whoa," blurted Riven. "Who punched you in the face? Was it Sky? Did you talk disrespectfully about chicks to him? You know that stuff doesn't fly with Sky . . ."

Riven wasn't tactful at the best of times, but today was really not his day. Matt's face darkened to match his eye.

"I was assaulted by that huge plant-pot in a dress."

"What, *Terra*?" Riven started to laugh in wildly surprised delight. Matt punched Riven, fist mashing Riven's lip against his teeth, and Riven choked on blood, still laughing.

"Yeah, Terra," snapped Matt. "Terra the crazy person! Or should I say, Terra the crazy three people at once."

Riven punched Matt as hard as he could. He swung his fist the way Sky had taught him, and he was amazed when Matt's head snapped back.

Then Matt cracked his neck and stared at Riven with murder in his eye. Riven fumbled for his dagger and realized he'd left it in his other shirt before he took the shirt off.

Wow, this terrible day was gonna end with Riven getting slaughtered.

He should try to talk Matt out of killing him. "Shut your mouth," Riven told Matt. "I'm not interested in half the garbage you say. I pretend I am so you'll think I'm cool."

Why was he talking like this! He hadn't known he had an actual death wish! Riven guessed it was sheer despair since he was getting murdered, anyway.

"I'm gonna break every bone in your loser body," promised Matt.

He took a step forward, and Riven's heart lurched. Then behind him, Sky yelled: "Catch, Riv!"

Riven spun, Specialist-fast, and caught the staff Sky had thrown him. Then he stared in complete indignation as Sky also handed Matt a staff.

"It has to be fair, Riv," Sky explained.

"It doesn't have to be fair, Sky!" Riven protested. "I was looking forward to having a fight rigged in my favor. Those are the only fights I wanna have!"

"You don't mean that," Sky said, and then made a face as if realizing something. "Wait, you really do."

"I really do!" Riven confirmed as Matt charged at him.

Matt wasn't actually that fast. Riven twisted out of the way, rolled, hit Matt in the knees with the staff, and watched him stagger. Incredibly, Matt's face when he looked at Riven was wary, as if he was facing an actual threat.

"You can do this," Sky encouraged.

"Feel free to jump in and beat him up with two-against-one odds anytime," said Riven.

"I would never do that!" Sky told him.

Like Riven didn't know that. Wow, Riven longed for two-against-one odds.

Riven sighed and treated Matt to a spinning kick in the chest. "You're so annoying."

He was better than Matt, Riven realized with dawning shock, but Matt was a lot bigger than he was, and it wasn't like Riven was a prodigy the way Sky was. This called for strategy. Riven feinted with the staff and saw Matt's eyes flicker. That was fear. Riven was intimately familiar with the feeling.

He feinted twice more, hit Matt once, got hit back so hard he saw stars, and then threw the staff into the air as he often tossed his dagger. When Matt was looking up at the staff, Riven launched himself at him and knocked him to the floor, canceling out Matt's height advantage and getting Matt by the throat. He fastened on to him, showing no mercy, until Matt tapped out.

Then Riven got up off Matt's chest, shaky with exhaustion and disbelief that he'd won. From now on, he was carrying two weapons around with him wherever he went. Riven's odds would always be two against one then.

When Matt clambered to his feet, he muttered, "It wasn't a fair fight."

"My guy, you are enormous," Riven informed him. "If I could've worked out how to cheat, I would absolutely have done it, but I didn't."

"We don't all get special training from perfect soldier boy Sky. Guess you pick your friends carefully," Matt said bitterly.

Riven's eyes slid, startled, to Sky. But Sky was still staring Matt down, face filled with righteous fury that Riven would have found deeply annoying . . . on any day but this day.

"Guess I do," said Riven.

Matt looked at Riven, leaning against the wall and wrecked, and Matt clearly had an idea about how to get his revenge. Riven barely had time to tense up before Sky got in Matt's way. Matt was armed and Sky wasn't, but Sky's grim face said that Matt should rethink his idea.

"Ugh," concluded Matt, and stalked off.

Using the staff Sky had given him, and his hand against the wall, Riven made his way to the steps and collapsed. After getting his breath back, he looked up and saw Sky looming over him like one of the imposing Specialist statues they had around the place. Riven hated showing weakness in front of people.

He knew it sounded ungrateful when he snapped, "Can't stop yourself from helping me out?"

"I could stop myself," said Sky, "but helping you was the right thing to do. Don't worry, you've made yourself clear. I know we're not friends."

"Right . . ." mumbled Riven. "I sure am saying a lot of stuff today!"

"True stuff," said Sky. "You've taken a truth potion made from the truthbells in the greenhouse. Here's the antidote."

He held out a small, violently blue vial. Riven recognized the seal on that vial. Terra had made this antidote. Had she done it for him? Or was she like Sky, helping because it was the right thing to do?

Why had Riven surrounded himself with do-gooders, anyway? He had to seriously reconsider his life choices. He had to find awful people to hang out with. Friends should have stuff in common.

"Thanks." Riven took the vial, broke the seal, uncapped it, and then hesitated. "Hey, Sky?"

"What?"

Sky had his hands behind his back. Still holding himself at attention in the dark with nobody else around, the perfect soldier boy. Sometimes Riven was jealous of him and sometimes he was irritated by him, but he didn't actually want to hurt Sky's feelings. Sky had been good to him. In a physically violent way that Riven had found difficult to interpret, but Riven got it now.

"Let's be friends," said Riven. "You know I mean it, because . . . truth potion."

Sky hesitated. "Why do you wanna be friends?"

Riven took the truth antidote like a shot. "Oh no, I think we've all had enough sincerity from Riven for one day! Now it's time to take advantage of our bond of undying manly friendship. Hey, help me up, *pal*, and then support me to the room. Also, get me a drink of water, *bro*. I'm dying here."

Sky sighed, but he grasped Riven's hand in a firm hold, and helped Riven to his feet. Once on his feet, Riven felt a sudden strange impulse that was almost like affection. For Sky? Matt must have hit him in the head even harder than he'd thought, but Riven went with it.

"Also thanks for not letting Matt kill me," he added, stepping in and giving Sky a loose, one-armed hug. "Bros don't let bros get murdered."

It was a bit like embracing a coatrack, except coatracks were more casual and relaxed. Sky just stood there, frozen in toy-soldier-got-broken mode.

"No to bro hugs?" Riven stepped back, raising his eyebrows. "Noted."

Riven tucked away the empty vial of the antidote Terra had made, winced, and tried not to remember everything he'd said today.

THE HEART GROWS OLD

Ben Harvey supervised as the future fairies and Specialists of Alfea climbed onto the bus after an extremely eventful Orientation Day. He hoped that he'd see them all back in a few months, that they hadn't been terrified away. They seemed like nice kids. Surely, some of them would be friends for his Terra.

"Thank you, Professor Harvey," said a girl with blue in her hair that was very fetching, and made her look like an iris.

He beamed at her and then cast an uneasy look at Callum Hunter, who'd been deputized to assist him.

Ben thought it was best for people to lean and grow toward the future, as plants leaned and grew toward the sun. The past was past and behind them. Still, Callum had given Ben coffees to give out to the kids, and then the kids had absolutely wilded out. Almost as though there had been something in the coffees.

"Did Farah really ask you to give Sky those coffees?" he asked.

Callum jumped. "I—of course! I wouldn't have dared do it otherwise."

Ben was silent. He could check with Farah. Maybe he would.

Callum bit his lip. "But I did add—I thought there was a comportment potion in your greenhouse, and I believed it might be a good idea to settle down some of the kids. It must have been truth potion. I'm sorry! I only wanted Orientation Day to go smoothly. If you tell Farah, maybe she'll fire me. That's all right. You should tell her. She should fire me. I deserve it."

Callum was sickly pale. It made Ben think of his own youth, and how scared he'd been once, during the wars.

"Well now," Ben said. "That was foolish, but we all make mistakes. I know that better than anyone. No harm done. I won't tell Farah."

He didn't want to see any young people suffering. Surely, Callum had learned his lesson, and he wouldn't be rash again.

Ben had taken every opportunity to impress his hard-earned lesson onto Sam: peace of mind and, tranquillity at all costs. He didn't want his son following the warrior's path. He feared that what he'd taught his boy, and what

Silva had taught his, conflicted too much for Sam and Sky to ever be friends—but if that was the price for peace, Ben would pay it.

Once when the kids were so young they probably didn't even remember, Ben and Silva let Sky, Sam, and Terra play together on the lawn. Playtime had quickly gotten out of hand. Little Terra made a dozen branches swing down on Sky at once, flailing at him like a murderous octopus while Sky hit out with a wooden sword and Terra yelled "Whack! Whack! Whack!" Sky, Terra, and Silva had all laughed uproariously. Sam had walked right through a tree to get away from the lunatics.

"You must be *very* proud of Terra," Silva said later.

He wasn't proud. It terrified Ben to see his children being prepared for war.

Ben said no more playdates, and Silva respected his wishes even if he didn't understand them. Saúl was always a loyal friend. Whenever Saúl and Farah chimed "Ben!" together in fond exasperation, Ben Harvey felt fully known and fully loved. Anyone would be lucky to have friends like these . . . but Ben wanted different friends and a different life for his kids.

He worried so much more about Terra than Sam. There was a glint in her eyes sometimes that made Ben want to put her under glass like an exotic plant that couldn't thrive in this land. But no. She was his sweet, shy little girl. Timid Terra and soft-spoken Sam would never think of flinging themselves into danger. They would never suffer as he had. He'd paid that price for them.

It was all worth it, for them to be safe.

One of the new kids was lingering at the door to the bus, listening to Ben and Callum. She was a girl in a plaid skirt, Terra's age but very unlike Terra in all other ways. She had sly dark eyes, Ben thought. He wondered what she'd heard.

"Get in the bus with you," said Ben, and the girl skipped up the bus steps and inside. "Go safely," he called after them.

Callum slunk off, but Ben watched as the vehicle rolled away through their gold-leaf gates and out into the world.

Farah and Saúl were driven by guilt, plagued by memories of the battles they had lost and won, but not Ben. He had to think of the future. He had to think of his children.

Were there children at Aster Dell?

There must have been. Ben knew how to read ashes and remains like rings on a tree, was familiar with the debris of history. There had been a baby's shoe, and a crushed shape almost like a cradle. There had been at least one, maybe two children in Aster Dell, he believed. Maybe more. Children as innocent as Sam and Terra. Children who might be the same age as Sam and Terra now, old enough to attend Alfea. If they had lived.

But they hadn't lived. Ben had to think of the living, and the future.

For his kids.

He went to bed and slept soundly, knowing he'd shown Farah's secretary some kindness. What Farah didn't know wouldn't hurt her.

Ben Harvey rose with the larks the next day, whistling and rolling up his sleeves, ready for some gardening. Yesterday had been frantic, but today would be peaceful, and hopefully every day after that. Peace in Alfea and all the realm, peace without end.

As he collected his gardening tools and walked away from the greenhouse with his mind on summer flowers, a boy knocked into his back, yelped at him, and then kept on running. Ben thought it was Riven, the horribly behaved Specialist boy who'd caused all the trouble yesterday. Silva must have his hands full with that kid. Sad, as Ben had thought the boy had promising pipette technique, but clearly he was a delinquent.

One day boys will be running like that to my Terra, he thought fondly. When Terra was old enough. Possibly when Terra was thirty.

And not any boys like that one. That boy had a knife.

"Don't run with knives!" he called after the boy.

Safety first. Ben never looked back at the past. Danger waited there.

Fairy Tale #6

*Education is not the filling of a pail, but
the lighting of a fire.*

—Plutarch

DO MOST BITTER WRONG

Dear Sir,

Good news! Though Orientation Day didn't go in the way I'd anticipated, I did succeed in dosing the three students with truth potion, and I confirmed beyond a shadow of a doubt that they have no idea what we're up to. Nobody in Alfea has the faintest notion of our plans. Not even the queen's own daughter.

I do understand your concerns about me giving the students truth potions, but there were no unfortunate consequences. I fooled Ben Harvey into believing I made a well-intentioned mistake, and he will cover for me. The arrogant fairies of Alfea are always underestimating humans. They will learn their mistake.

I ask for your patience. I really believe this has all turned out for the best. Now that I know that I'm not suspected, I can continue with our great work. Rest assured, soon I will have the key to Dowling's secrets and our victory.

I have reason to believe Dowling found something in the First World. I will write more as soon as I get the chance.

Yours,

Callum Hunter

MIND

As the bus drove away from Alfea, Musa was startled when Aisha chose the seat beside hers.

"Is this okay?" Aisha's mind was open and relaxed, and Musa was glad she'd thought to ask.

"If you don't mind that I'm not very chatty," warned Musa.

Aisha promised, "I don't mind."

"Well, wasn't that an interesting excursion," murmured Beatrix, who was sitting next to that boy Dane.

He seemed taken aback but charmed by Beatrix's presence beside him. Musa was glad they'd found each other, she guessed. She didn't like either of their minds much.

Aisha's mind, now that her worries had calmed down, was far more pleasant. Musa didn't dislike having Aisha sitting next to her, Aisha's thoughts running along like a river coursing determinedly to its destination. Aisha respected the headphones, and when she offered a bag of healthy snacks Musa turned them down, but she pushed the headphones slightly off her ears before she did so, indicating willingness to talk. Musa's power allowed her so few boundaries that it made her like people who respected what boundaries she could keep.

"So that was Alfea," Aisha said. "What did you think?"

"Someone told me that they went to Alfea so they could learn how to be a hero," Musa contributed. "I have to say, nobody at Alfea seemed as if they were feeling all that heroic today."

"I don't know if heroic is something you ever feel," Aisha said thoughtfully. "I think being heroic is something you try to be. That's why I want to go to Alfea. I want to get all the tools I need so I'll be able to try as hard as I can. Does that make sense?"

Musa made a so-so gesture. "Eh."

She wanted to think about what Aisha had said, so she slipped her headphones back on and listened to her music. Behind her Beatrix and Dane whispered conspiratorially, her braided head close to his buzzed one, and Musa could have listened in to their minds but chose not to. Beside her, Aisha wrote up a schedule that seemed complicated, and involved a frightening amount of swimming and dedicated study. Aisha was radiating determination.

The bus rolled on, through the woods and hills in the evening, the realm of Solaria silver as the sea under the moon.

"See you at Alfea," Aisha told Musa with a grin when her stop eventually came. "I mean . . . I hope I will."

Musa considered again what Aisha had said to her. About not feeling heroic, but trying to be. Clearly, Aisha was trying. Musa could try, too, in her own way. Maybe everyone at Alfea was trying, soldier boy Sky and terrible Riven, terrifying princess Stella and that annoying flower girl. Even Headmistress Dowling and Specialist Headmaster Silva. Everyone.

Musa kind of liked the idea of stepping out of her world of whirling emotions into action.

Her mother was dead, her last impression on the world pain echoing in Musa's mind that she couldn't forget, but Musa was alive. Where else could Musa go? What else could she do? She might as well try.

Musa grinned back, and came to a decision. "See you at Alfea."

Aisha exited the bus in one long-legged athletic leap, blue-and-black hair trailing after her like a river. She called over her shoulder, "Looking forward to it!"

Musa leaned back in her seat and let the feeling wash over her again, the emotion even more precious because it could not be kept: peace. Even better, hope for peace in the future.

SPECIALIST

Sky finished his dawn circuit of Alfea, stopping in front of the castle. The sun was striking the windows with gold, the sky blazing blue over the rooftops. Today might be a less complicated day than yesterday.

The Specialists' lakes were filled with simple blue as well. The mirrors of the sky, Stella had told him the lakes were called. The first time Silva said Sky was growing up to look just like his dad, Sky had gone and stared at his reflection in one of the Specialists' lakes, searching for his father. He'd stirred up the waters with a staff so the surface was disturbed and the reflection distorted. All he could see was a tall fair-haired figure with his face in darkness, standing with the light behind him. His reflection hadn't seemed like a dad.

On a platform spanning the lake, Silva was going through passes with a staff. Sky tried to run discreetly past.

"Sky!" Silva called. "Hey, boy. I know you can hear me. Come over here now."

Pretend you didn't hear him and keep running! suggested the voice in Sky's head that was beginning to sound like Riven, but naturally Sky would never dream of disobeying Silva's orders.

He walked over to the lakes, every step heavy as Sky's shame about all the stuff he'd said yesterday. Silva must think he was pathetic, not soldier material.

Silva stared at a point over Sky's head. "So yesterday was a mess."

"Uh," Sky said. "Yeah. Sorry, sir. I was dosed with truth potion. Terra did it, I think."

Silva frowned. "Terra did it? Why?"

"Not sure," Sky mumbled. "She was annoyed with me, apparently? All a misunderstanding."

Silva shook his head.

"Little killer," he said fondly, and Sky knew Silva wouldn't get Terra into trouble. Silva admired dangerous things, like the fairy horse Professor Harvey had been nursing once, the steed that ate human flesh. "Never mind that. Truth's no bad thing. But what on earth were your friends thinking, embarrassing Ms. Dowling?"

There was no doubt, between "killing someone stone dead" and "mildly inconveniencing Ms. Dowling," which Silva considered the bigger sin.

"Uh," said Sky guiltily.

"Do you enjoy spending your leisure hours discussing Ms. Dowling's private life?" Silva snapped. "Have any more weird theories you want to share?"

Sky shook his head. "No, sir!"

After a long moment in which Silva eyed Sky with dark suspicion, Silva's bristling reduced a fraction, and Sky knew he was being let off.

"You'd better not," Silva grumbled.

"Sometimes when Stella or Riven talk, I just let it wash over me without paying attention to the details," Sky confessed. The details could get distressing.

Silva grunted. "Well. That's understandable. Would probably do the same, if I had to spend significant time with Stella or Riven."

Sky was torn between pleasure that Silva had indicated he and Sky were alike, which he hardly ever did and which

Sky always wanted to hear, and the distinct feeling that Sky should defend his friends when they were insulted.

"That light magic of Stella's was a bit too strong yesterday," Silva continued. "I don't like seeing a weapon in the hands of someone who'll misuse it. That girl is growing up to be the image of her mother."

Sky wouldn't contradict Silva for himself, but he wheeled on Silva then. He laid a firm hand on his arm so Silva lowered his staff and Sky met his eyes. He remembered Stella's tear-wet, star-bright blue eyes last night, looking trustfully up at Sky. He held Silva's gaze, letting him know that he truly meant it.

"No, she's not," Sky promised. "Stella's never going to be anything like her mother. I believe in her."

Silva took a step back as he always did, but he nodded. "If you say so, Sky."

Sky cast an eye toward the rack of weapons, then the chestnut trees, and back again. While he was risking Silva's displeasure, he might as well go all the way.

"And . . . I'm gonna ask Riven to be roommates with me again next year. I know Riven's not a hero or anything, like you and Dad," Sky said awkwardly. "I don't take him seriously. But . . ."

That was the whole point. It was nice, to be able to not take something seriously for a change. It was cool, sometimes, to believe even Sky could relax and have fun.

Sky shrugged uncomfortably. "I just want to."

Silva drew in a deep breath, as though trying to gather his patience, and Sky waited in dread to be yelled at.

"Do what you want, then. You're a loyal friend," said Silva. "I'm proud of you."

Was he really? That was unexpected, but good. Sky always tried to make Silva proud. Pride was almost love.

Sky nodded. "Thank you, sir."

The sun climbed higher and brighter and everything seemed pretty good, for a moment. Then everything went wrong.

"After you'd taken that truth potion, you said . . . some things," Silva said haltingly. "You got pretty upset. I'm a simple man. Lived my whole life with a sword in my hand. I'm not the best at . . . feelings, or talking about them, but if you were unhappy, you'd tell me. Right?"

He stood beside Sky, smaller than Sky was now, squinting against the sun.

Silva might have lived his whole life with a sword in his hand, but Sky had lived his life with a sword on his back. Ready for the battle that Silva was certain he'd have to fight, carrying the legacy of the past and Silva's dread for the future on his shoulders.

Sky squared those shoulders now. He'd been raised a soldier. He could be brave without a truth potion. "I do wonder sometimes . . . Are you ever sorry you took me in?"

There was a long silence as Silva considered his words.

He was always careful with what he said to Sky, and Sky always believed whatever he said.

"I'm sorry for a lot of things," said Silva at last. "Guess I should be sorry for that one as well. Funny thing, though. I'm not sorry, Sky. I'm never gonna be sorry." He paused, then asked unexpectedly, "You sorry I did? It's all right if you are."

Sky stood to attention. "No, sir."

"It'd make sense if you were," Silva told him. "You would've been brought up in luxury in Eraklyon. You didn't have to be dragged around the fairy realms and battered with endless training by a rough old soldier."

"I'm not sorry!" exclaimed Sky. "I'm like you. I'm never going to be sorry."

A small smile stole over Silva's face, and Sky basked in his approval. Sky might be a little taller than Silva these days, but he always looked up to him.

"Well, all right, then," said Silva, and Sky took it as dismissal and moved to leave the platform. He didn't want to bother Silva. He'd already got away with enough.

"Hey, Sky!" Silva snapped, and Sky turned back fast, at attention. "Come back here."

When Sky did, Silva was staring at the lake waters, not at him. Then Silva reached out.

Silva wasn't much for hugs. Actually, he'd never hugged Sky, though he would hug Sky back on the rare times Sky got up the nerve to hug him. But sometimes when he got in Sky's face, he would press his forehead against Sky's forehead, to emphasize that he truly meant what he said.

Often what Silva meant was that Sky needed to stop favoring his left.

He did that now, collaring Sky by the scruff as though he was a misbehaving puppy, shaking him a little and knocking their foreheads together, brief and too hard. "When it comes to what really matters . . ." Silva said roughly.

Sky couldn't understand or remember for an instant. Then his own disastrous truth came rushing back to him. Sky remembered exactly what he'd asked Silva yesterday, about his dad and about Sky himself.

Did you care about him? Do you care about me?

Silva swallowed, a grating sound in a dry throat. "I did," he said. "I did, I did . . . and I do."

"And I—" began Sky, feeling tears start in his eyes.

Silva disengaged fast, shoving Sky back. "Think that's enough of that!" he announced. "Can we get in a little staff practice before class? You've been sloppy lately, boy."

"Of course," said Sky. "Sorry, sir."

"Come at me."

Silva gestured Sky in, and Sky smiled as he twirled a staff around, ready for the fight.

"Coming in strong," he promised.

In the heaven-blue mirror of the sky that was the lake,

moving across the platform bearing the insignia of Alfea, two figures fell into the patterns of combat. One was dark and sturdy, one was golden and tall, but they moved in the exact same way.

If Sky had been looking at their reflections then, he might have seen what he wanted to see.

SPECIALIST

Usually when the door slid shut on Sky leaving for one of his masochistic dawn runs, Riven rolled over and put his head under a pillow with the smug conviction that his life was at least briefly better than Sky's. Today he waited until the sound of Sky's footsteps had faded away, then rolled out of bed and climbed into his clothes.

On his way out the door, he grabbed his knife and tossed it, caught it neatly without even thinking, and looked at the gleaming thing in his hands with mild surprise. Right. He'd take that as a good luck sign.

Riven made his way, as he had so many times this year before and after class, to the greenhouse. He almost collided with Terra's dad on the path there, rebounding off Professor Harvey and throwing an apology over his shoulder. He was in a hurry.

He found Terra in the greenhouse already, busily pruning the hanging ferns. The box of truthbells was closed and padlocked.

Riven stopped at the door. There were about fourteen marble tiles between them, but she seemed farther away than that.

"Hi," Riven said when Terra didn't speak.

"Hello, Riven," Terra responded distantly, pruning her ferns. "What are you doing here?"

"Sky told me you gave him the antidote to the truth potion," said Riven. "So about what I was saying under the influence of the potion, I'm—"

"Oh, did Sky give it to you?" Terra asked. "I made the antidote for him. He's such a good guy, isn't he? Sky. Legit one of the best. But you wouldn't know that much about good guys, would you, Riven?"

She looked at him directly then. Terra's gaze had always been soft and sympathetic whenever she saw Riven, from the first time when she found him crying in the greenhouse under a flowering tree. It was as though she always perceived him through a veil, blurring his many imperfections so she could see the best of him.

The veil had been well and truly ripped away now. Terra watched him with clear eyes, the same way Sky or Silva did when Riven fumbled and dropped a weapon. The way the gorgeous Mind Fairy in purple had yesterday, seeing right through him, her lips curling in distaste.

Nobody was impressed. But was Riven impressive?

Riven smirked, tossing his knife in the air. "Guess not."

"Why did you come here, Riven?" Terra asked. "Did you imagine I'd want you to come, after knowing the truth about how you see me? You actually believed I'd swallow the insult and keep feeding your ego by fussing over you? Wow. You must think I have no pride at all. I didn't realize you found me *that* pathetic."

Riven took a step forward to show he wasn't in the least intimidated. His own face flashed in the windowpane in front of him, emerging from among the hanging leaves, a little pale.

"Yeah," he told the glass. "You're pretty pathetic."

They had both been pathetic this year, he guessed. Seeing what they wanted to see, each of them lonely enough to fool themselves. Terra in the greenhouse under a shining rain of truth. Terra, who'd believed Riven was a good guy. But not anymore.

"You can go now, Riven," Terra said, and her voice was a sword.

"Suits me." Riven turned away. "I've got better places to be."

He could go back to the greenhouse later, if he wanted to find any recreational plants. That was all the place was good for, anyway. He headed down to the Specialists' lakes. Maybe he could get some early-morning practice in, like Sky. He realized he'd been absentmindedly tossing and catching his knife without fumbling as he walked. Maybe he was a martial arts genius!

Silva and Sky were already on a platform, talking intently. He'd grab a staff and join them.

"I know Riven's not a hero, or anything, like you and Dad," he heard Sky tell Silva. "I don't take him seriously."

Riven veered away from the platforms and the lake. Or maybe not being a dedicated soldier! Maybe that was the dumbest plan Riven had ever had! Back to the recreational plants idea.

He was going to have fun for a change, that was what he was going to do. Matt was *right* about Terra. Everything Matt had said was right. Terra was a weird loner, and Riven was done being pathetic. He was going to have drinks with awesome guys, and he was going to hook up with cute girls. Surely, he could find a girl who liked his mean jokes, and a guy who thought Riven was cool. Having fun was a life plan. Being the gigolo of the fairy realms honestly sounded a lot better than being a Specialist.

Riven didn't have to take himself seriously, any more than Sky did. Who cared about not fitting into the box Alfea had prepared for him? He was going to chill out. If he found oblivion in any of the many recreational activities open to him, he wouldn't have to think about anyone's opinion of him. Not even his own.

There was a flask of booze in Riven and Sky's room, left over from the Senior Specialists' party. Riven went back to their room, propped his feet on the desk, and tossed back the contents of the flask.

His throat was still burning when Sky entered the room.

Sky blinked. "Uh, what're you doing, Riv?"

Riven bared his teeth. "Just having fun."

Sky seemed puzzled, but he shook his head and grinned, relenting. Maybe because they were friends now.

I don't take him seriously, said Sky's voice in Riven's mind, but Riven relented, too, taking the bared teeth down a notch so it was a grin back. How could he blame Sky? At least Sky was still willing to put up with him.

"Hey, Riv," said Sky. "I was wondering if you wanted to be roommates next year?"

"Yeah," Riven confirmed nonchalantly. "Sounds cool."

There was a pause. Riven glanced over his shoulder and saw Sky was smiling to himself a bit. Cold misery was washed away, inch by inch, by creeping warmth at the realization that Sky had picked Riven, despite Riven not being a hero. Maybe it didn't matter what Sky really thought about him. It wasn't as if Sky had got it wrong.

"Let's commemorate this moment," proposed Riven, and produced his phone. "Bro selfie."

He held up his arm and Sky came willingly. Riven threw his arm around Sky's neck and tried a few different angles with his phone. Sadly, Sky seemed to have no bad angles.

"Should I make a sign like some people do in their Instagram pictures?" Sky asked.

"Do you mean a peace sign?"

Sky looked taken aback. "Is there a war sign?"

Many temptations arose at this point. It was so clear Riven had to instantly say yes, make up a war sign, then get Sky to do it and immortalize this moment forever on the 'gram.

He looked into Sky's earnest, hopeful face and couldn't make himself do it. Terra was right about Sky, the same way she was right about Riven. Sky was a good guy. The best.

"Just sit there and look pretty, bud," Riven advised. He lifted his phone and snapped his first selfie with Sky in it.

Then he checked the selfie. Riven looked weird in this picture. Maybe he'd look weird in any picture next to Sky. Maybe this picture was only the first installment in Riven's future of inferiority as Sky's friend.

He kind of wanted to delete it.

He posted the photo on Instagram anyway, with the caption "Good news, ladies: It's official. Get ready to cast your votes for the best-looking roomies in Alfea for the second year running."

"Is your caption disrespectful to women?" Sky's voice was suspicious.

Riven winked. "Would I ever, Sky? You wound me."

"Oh no, Riven, why, why—"

Underneath the picture, comments started to appear. Riven read them with a sinking feeling of inevitability.

Imagine being roommates with Sky . . . JEALOUS!

Who is THAT with several fire emojis.

Lucky! you not him hehe

Delete that picture, Riven's mind ordered him. *Just delete it.* Instead he turned off the comments. If he didn't have to see the comments, he didn't have to think about everyone else's low opinion of him. He was planning on oblivion for the rest of this year. He might as well get started now.

It would all be different next year. He'd be different next year. He'd be friends with Sky, but he'd make other friends, too. He'd get a girlfriend. Not a demented one like Stella, a cool one. He and Sky would be equals, someday soon. More important than anything else, there would be no more hanging out in the greenhouse like a loser.

Riven nodded to himself with decision, getting up to slide his phone in one pocket and his silver flask in the other. He'd fill up the flask again later today, when he got the chance.

As he did so, he tossed his knife again, his eyes following the path of the blade, shining on the way up and the way down. He reached out and grabbed it, the reflex coming easy to him now, after all this practice. Knife caught, held, and balanced. For now.

The next instant, Riven dropped his knife on the floor. He blamed Sky for this, since Sky had chosen this particular moment to step up to Riven and give him a swift, nervous hug, moving stiffly as though maybe Sky hadn't hugged many people before in his whole life.

"Yes to bro hugs," Sky told him.

Riven thumped Sky on the back as he returned the hug, and found himself actually smiling. He hid the smile in Sky's shoulder so nobody would see. "Noted."

WATER

Before Aisha went home, there was one last thing she had to do. Long ago, she'd made a resolution to swim twice every day, and when Aisha decided something, she never swerved. Every day meant every day.

No matter how weird that day had been.

Aisha loved water in all its forms, but after the woodland streams and warriors' pools and alarming fountains of Alfea, she had a destination in mind. She kicked off her shoes, climbed over the dunes, and headed down toward the sea.

When the ocean was laid out at her feet, sunlight catching the water so it glittered like treasure placed before a princess, Aisha sighed and finally let herself relax.

She shimmied out of her peacock-blue-and-purple midi dress and left it behind her in a little pool of fabric on the sands. The water claimed her as she walked in, step-by-step into another world, and finally dived under the surface. She was in her element at last.

Aisha loved swimming pools, training with teammates, and clearly marked lines so you knew precisely where to go. But there were times when a girl needed the ocean. The sound of the wind over the sea had been Aisha's first lullaby. She'd learned to swim in the sea, setting records against herself and breaking them and calling out her victory to the waves. Today, she wanted to break the speed record she'd set last month.

As she struck out into the deep blue, her mind traveled back to the deep green forest. Aisha considered the prospect of future teammates at Alfea. She already liked Musa and thought she could see ways to help Musa get through school already. All Musa needed was low-pressure company. Aisha didn't trust Stella or Beatrix, but she'd noticed Terra the Earth Fairy trying persistently to help out and talk to people. Aisha appreciated team spirit. She thought Terra could definitely be a friend. Maybe Aisha would end up rooming with Musa or Terra? That would be great.

The key thing at Alfea would be a roommate she could get along with. Aisha would put in the effort, and they'd be a team. Unless they were someone terrible, or they didn't want to be friends, or they looked down on Aisha for not having total control of her magic yet.

She felt another twinge of dread, leaping and churning in her as her power had twisted out of control at the fountain today. Then Aisha remembered Ms. Dowling and her absolute steadiness in the face of strange powers.

She didn't let her strokes falter. She cut her way across the waves and won the race against herself. When she surfaced, she did so in a burst of sea spray, face uplifted to the sky. Everything was triumphant blue on blue.

Aisha wanted teammates, but if she had to, she could strike out alone. She believed in her power. She had to be on her own team first.

In time, a drip of water could bore through stone. A river changing course could change the land. The sea could eat up a shore. One day, a raindrop would become the ocean.

Aisha stayed winning.

EARTH

The door of the greenhouse slid open, and Terra choked off her sobs and scrubbed at the dirt and tears on her face. If that was Riven coming back to grovel and beg her forgiveness . . . well, she'd never forgive him, she would haughtily scorn him, of course, but if it was . . .

It wasn't Riven. It was Sam.

"Oh," said Terra, and burst into fresh tears.

Her brother looked terrified, but he hurried over all the same and sat with her, arm around her shoulders in the mud beneath the ferns. They'd always got grubby, gardening together. Terra was ten before she knew that Sam's freckles weren't just dirt.

She and her brother weren't much alike, but they had the same freckles.

"Did that Specialist guy bother you?"

"What?" asked Terra, in dismay, then remembered that Sam meant that other Specialist.

Calm, good-humored Sam had a murderous expression on his face. That surprised Terra, and anyway Sam had got everything wrong, but it was nice to know he cared.

Terra patted Sam's arm. "Who cares about that guy? I beat him up with some trees and had the pond weed grab him and dunk him a bunch."

Sam was the only person in Alfea who wouldn't have been surprised by this information. Her brother raised his eyebrows slightly, and then sighed and accepted it. "Don't know how I'm gonna face Dad when you go to jail for murdering someone with a plant."

"Don't be silly, Sam," said Terra. "Murder is wrong. If I ever kill anyone with a plant, it will be for a good reason. Like self-defense, or if they were evil—and I would attempt to restrain or subdue them first, obviously. I would not use a poisonous plant with lethal intent—that would be deeply irresponsible. I would use vines, or potentially branches if they could lift the person aloft, or aquatic plants if water was involved, but I wouldn't hold them under the surface long enough to cause brain damage. Anyway, that would be a good deed, so I shouldn't be jailed for it."

Sam nudged her. "Given it a lot of thought, have we? If that guy didn't upset you, then why were you crying?"

Why are you crying? Terra turned her head so Sam wouldn't see, and had the tender fronds of a fern whisk away a last tear.

"Guess I was just feeling a little lonely," she told him.

"Aw, Terra," Sam said, his shoulders collapsing as he sighed, "I'm really sorry. I've been a garbage brother this year, haven't I?"

There was a silence. Terra wasn't planning to contradict him. He'd been her partner in crime all their lives, with no other kids around when they were growing up except Sky shining in the distance. Then suddenly Terra had been all alone, and she'd fallen in with bad company and made some very bad decisions! Some relating to sword-sized thorn-bushes.

The glass and stone of the greenhouse, the fronds of plants and hanging baskets dangling from the ceiling, the tiny cacti and huge potted ferns, surrounded her. Their familiarity was like an embrace. This was Terra's place of power, and nobody was going to spoil it or sully it for her.

Sam was the same as the greenhouse to her, a familiar and well-loved sight in his worn green jacket, his dark hair gelled to one side because he was trying to look cool.

It occurred to her that Sam's hair had always been messy,

before this year. Maybe Terra wasn't the only Harvey sibling anxious to fit in.

"You're not a garbage brother usually," Terra assured him finally. "Always pretty irritating, of course."

"You're not the only one who dreamed of finally being able to go to Alfea," said Sam. "And yeah, honestly, when I thought of hanging with the guys, or going on a date with a hot girl, I didn't imagine my little sister figuring hugely into the picture. Do you imagine me there when you finally have an all girls' club in a tree house?"

"No," Terra admitted. "There would be a sign forbidding you to come in."

She'd actually already made a clubhouse that Sam had been barred from so she could play tea parties with her dolls in peace. Her friends had been imaginary then. They were still imaginary now, she supposed.

Did plants count as imaginary friends? Terra's friends were plants.

But next year, her friends wouldn't be imaginary. They would be people, not plants. Terra paused as a total brainwave hit, rocking her with the force of her own genius. She would gift her new friends with plants. That was a surefire way to make them like her! Next year, for sure.

Until then, she guessed she had her annoying brother.

"It was wrong of me not to check in on you," Sam admitted. "I had no idea you were getting preyed on by Specialist creeps! I thought you'd be okay, pottering around in the greenhouse like always. I thought I could take some time to, you know, make friends. Date."

A canna plant offered Terra a large, paddle-like leaf. Terra gratefully blew her nose into it. Sam gave her a judgmental look for being gross, but she wasn't being gross—she was being at one with nature!

"Can't blame you for trying to date before you inevitably go bald like Dad," Terra told him.

Sam shoved her. "Why do you always have to bring that up—it might not happen—"

"It will happen! It's bound to happen. It's coming like sprouts in spring." Terra wrinkled her nose. "Is that why you're trying to do your hair fancy these days? Hey, I get it. Enjoy hair while you still have it, Sam!"

"Anyway, I'm going back to ignoring you," Sam announced.

Terra quit laughing. Teasing was still too sharp between them, the hurt too fresh, so every time Sam brushed up against a sore point, Terra wanted to snap at him.

Sam put his arm around her shoulder and squeezed. "Just kidding. Got your back, Sis."

He hadn't had her back. But Sam had come to her when she was crying. He was with her now, even if he'd thought she was too big a loser to hang around with all year. He was right. Everybody thought Terra was a loser. What mattered was that Sam still loved her. And she loved him.

"You're a big annoying twerp," Terra told him lovingly. "And you didn't even get a girlfriend. No surprise there!"

Sam grabbed up a fistful of soil and tried to put it down the back of Terra's Peter Pan collar. Terra fought him off, ferns getting in a few slaps at him for her. Terra's earth magic had always been more aggressive. Sam was a child of peace and nature, which was why he was going down hard.

"I did not vibe with any of the girls in my year once I got to know them," said Sam loftily, once he'd smacked down several ferns. "It was entirely a matter of choice."

Terra snorted. "Sure." She hesitated. "I didn't vibe with anybody at Orientation Day," she confessed in a tiny voice. "Not in a friend way, I mean. What—what if I never make any friends at all?"

Sam hugged her. Terra put her head down on her big brother's shoulder and sniffled.

"You will," Sam promised in her ear. "Even though you're a total worrywart mess, I promise you that you will." He paused. "And maybe one of your roommates will be hot, and you can put in a good word for me."

Terra hit Sam. "Stay away from me and all my friends next year! Back off! My friends are going to be amazing, and you're not allowed to bother them!"

Sam cracked a smile, while she belabored him with her fists. Even though her eyes were still damp, sitting in the rich earth with her brother and the scent of jasmine, Terra found herself able to smile, too.

LIGHT

The day after Orientation Day was bright and beautiful, and Stella was planning to have lunch with Sky and Ricki because the rest of her suitemates were in disgrace. They were crawling to make it up to her, and perhaps she would let them, but for now Stella wanted to be with the people she trusted.

She regarded her exclusive table and the gorgeous faces at it with supreme satisfaction. When her gaze hit the lone sulky weasel face, her smile slipped, but she fastened it firmly in place.

Almost everything was lovely. It was sad Riven was here, but Stella supposed life couldn't be perfect. Not until she was queen and could exile Riven from this land.

"My favorite people," she declared, setting her tray down on the lunch table beside Ricki's. ". . . And Riven."

Riven toasted to her with a silver flask, which he then tipped up to his mouth.

"Are you—" Stella couldn't believe her eyes. "Are you drinking in the cafeteria, at lunchtime, is that actually what's happening here?"

"You inspire me, Princess," said Riven.

Stella turned her gaze to the black-and-white photographs of notable Alfea students who had to witness Riven defiling their hallowed halls.

Sky was watching Riven with a troubled air. "That isn't super good for your reflexes, Riv. Or for you generally."

"Specialists need healthy livers," agreed Ricki. "What if you had an unhealthy liver and then someone stabbed you in it?"

She smiled her infectious smile, and Stella and Sky both smiled, too. Only Riven, who had a horrible nature, didn't smile for Ricki. His face was even more unpleasant than usual, Stella reflected. Looking at him now, she couldn't imagine how she'd ever believed he could be a suitable partner for Ricki.

"I'm just having fun," he said, wearing the most sour and miserable expression imaginable.

Stella rolled her eyes. "Gracious me, I don't care about your emotional or physical well-being! I focus on the important things in life. Think of how your behavior makes *me* look, Riven."

He scowled at her. She sneered at him. She had to come up with a new plan for Riven. She supposed she would simply have to regard him as though Sky had adopted an incontinent dog out of a misguided charitable impulse. *Sorry about him, I know he's not cute. My boyfriend's good heart really is, though, isn't it?*

Stella nodded decisively to herself. She thought that would work. And she would scour the school for Ricki and find her a better man. There had to be somebody. Though nobody was as good as Sky. It was such a pity that Sky was a tragic orphan and didn't have a cute brother for Ricki.

She glanced covertly around. Thanks to the little chandelier of light she'd placed above the table, she knew they all looked good. Nobody appeared to have noticed the fact Riven was a delinquent mess. People were staring at her with admiration and envy. When Stella reached out and touched Sky's hand, the envy on several girls' faces became more pronounced.

Really, now Stella was reflecting on Sky's wonderful nature and other people's inherent untrustworthiness, she supposed she should start watching out and stop other girls from getting all up in Sky's business. Except for Ricki, of course. She had absolute faith in Ricki.

"Let's concentrate on the important things. Everyone agrees that the decorations for Orientation Day were fabulous," said Ricki enthusiastically. "Here's to the princess."

She lifted a glass of sparkling apple juice. Sky, smiling in the easy way he did when Ricki was around, clinked his glass of juice against hers.

"To the princess," he said softly.

Riven pretended to barf. Stella supposed that was on brand. She ignored Riven completely, and gave Sky and Ricki a fond look.

"Let's toast to nonroyal people, too. We cannot forget about them, 'cause, you know, they can be pretty cute."

She twinkled over at Sky, with his hair that wanted to fall in a wheaten sheaf into his steadfast dark blue eyes. She was going to appreciate him more, and Ricki, too. She leaned over the table and gave Sky a kiss.

Riven's pretend barfing intensified.

"Obviously, when I was talking about nonroyal people I appreciated, I didn't mean you, Riven," said Stella when she leaned back.

"If you did think I was cute," said Riven, "I would be forced to fake my own death."

"Guys, you're going to have to learn to get along sometime," Sky said.

Stella and Riven shook their heads, in accord. Sky was such a beautiful soul, for whom hope always triumphed over realism, but Stella shouldn't enable his delusions of goodwill among men.

"You are," Sky insisted. "Since I asked Riven if he wanted to be roommates again next year, and he said he did, and so you two will be seeing a lot of each other—"

"I'm rethinking being roommates, I'm rethinking everything," said Riven, and Sky started to rain down blows on him.

Riven scuffled at him in return, feeble but vicious.

"I'm horrified to hear that you've made this terrible decision, Sky," Stella told him truthfully, "but you remind me that I have a very important piece of business to conclude. Ricki, we're going to be roommates next year, aren't we?"

As she spoke, she felt a sudden qualm of unexpected nerves. What if Ricki didn't want to, after all the events of Orientation Day? Stella wouldn't want to room with anybody who would plot against her.

She didn't have to wait in suspense long. Ricki squealed with joy and dived at Stella.

Since boys were uncivilized, Sky and Riven were expressing their affections by beating on each other, wrestling until Riven fell off the bench onto the cobblestones. Stella, a supremely civilized princess, put her arm around Ricki's shoulder.

Ricki's face shone. "I'd love to, Stella! Are you sure you want to?"

"Naturally, I'm sure," said Stella. "Aren't I always sure? Aren't you my best friend?"

Ricki nodded enthusiastically, arms around Stella's waist, and laid her head against Stella's shoulder. Stella hid her own smile in Ricki's hair, not wanting to show how thrilled and relieved she was.

It was settled. They would be roommates, and best friends forever. Sky would stay by her side and be loyal always.

Ms. Dowling didn't know what she was saying when she warned Stella that her magic was out of control. Ms. Dowling was underestimating Stella, the way Queen Luna always did.

No, not the way Queen Luna did. Stella was sure now that if she was in trouble, Ms. Dowling would help her.

The thing was, it wouldn't be necessary. Yesterday had been an anomaly. Stella wasn't ever going to need anybody's help again.

She gazed down the hall, through to stone archways and open doors. So many places in Alfea were entryways of opportunity.

Stella could see the golden path of the future before her as though it stretched before her eyes, lit with her own magic.

She would be admired, and beloved, and practically perfect in every way. She would take care of Ricki, and make sure she was the most glorious girl in school. Next to Stella, of course.

She would finish the year in style, and her next year in Alfea would be even more glorious than the first.

Stella took a sip of sparkling apple juice, turned to liquid gold by her light, and oh, it tasted sweet. She echoed her best friend's toast silently in her mind.

Here's to the princess.

THE HEART
GROWS OLD

"I admit that orientation was an experiment I may not be interested in repeating, but the whole business is a little funny when you think about it," said Farah, installed back in the headmistress's office after a very long Orientation Day, followed by an even longer day of clearing up its aftereffects.

Stella and Aisha's little trick with the fountain had actually created a hole in the hedge that it had taken her and Ben some time to repair.

Farah leaned back in the carved chair behind her desk and sighed. She noted Specialist Headmaster Silva, her second-in-command and the second-most-important person in Alfea, was half lying in one of her brown leather armchairs and tossing a knife up into the air to amuse himself, like a boy.

Silva raised his eyebrows. "The students making disgusting suggestions about your personal life is funny?" He seemed far more offended by that matter than she was.

Now that she was off duty—though Farah never felt she was entirely off duty—she didn't have to stay behind the desk. She came out from behind it and sank into the seat beside Silva's. The table beside the sofa was actually a chest in which she kept her battle armor, but she hadn't opened it in years. She set a drink on it now.

"Think about all that we worried about when we were their age," said Farah. "I like that they're able to be young fools."

"Do they have to be *such* fools, though? I'd prefer a bit less foolishness, personally," Silva grumbled. "There are limits."

Farah surveyed her office with quiet pleasure. Once it had been Rosalind's domain, solemn under mahogany rafters, but Farah liked to think she'd made good changes. It was Farah's room now, painted in her favorite shade of blue, with gold stenciling around the circular shapes of the windows. She'd installed more shelves along the walls up to the ceiling, filling them with battered books and volumes with gilt spines, decorated them with potted plants Ben had given her that he said made him think of her. The plants were subdued colors, and sturdy with deep roots. Farah took the plants as a compliment. She cherished those plants, watered them, turned them toward the light, and tried to make sure they would thrive.

"Did you find whatever it was you ran off looking for?" Silva asked now, with one eye on her and one eye on his knife. She didn't think the question was as casual as he tried to make it sound.

"I'm . . . not sure," said Farah. "I found nothing certain. Perhaps there is nothing to be found. I may have to return to the First World and look again."

"Send me," Silva volunteered instantly.

Farah shook her head. "If there is a secret of Rosalind's in the First World, then it is magic. I am a fairy and can fight magic with magic. If I see a monster, I'll point you and your sword toward it, but this is my problem. What would you say to me if I asked you to go into danger I wasn't willing to face?"

Silva seemed faintly bemused by the question, as if she should already know the answer. He stopped tossing his knife, tucking it away into one of the many hiding places for weapons in his dark jacket.

He told her, "I'd say 'As you command.'"

"Oh, no doubt." Farah gave a light laugh, turning the matter aside. "In any case, I have my own feet and my own magic. Trust me to go into danger on my own, and come back, too. I went this time, and it wasn't so bad, was it? Confess, you hardly noticed I was gone."

A dry joke and a little self-deprecation, and they could leave this strange moment behind them.

She'd asked for enough, from Saúl and Ben both, in this lifetime. She'd go to them for the sake of Alfea, of course, but she wished she could handle all the responsibility herself.

Silva's eyes were on her, very blue and very serious.

"I noticed. Everybody noticed. You're the beating heart of this school, Farah," said Saúl. "Can't help but notice when your heart skips a beat."

"Oh," said Farah uncertainly. This wasn't like Saúl. "Come now. No need to act as if you can't do without me."

"I can't do without you," said Saúl simply.

No. She supposed she couldn't do without him or Ben, either. They were bonded forever, the three souls who had walked away alive from Aster Dell. But they never talked about that.

"How is Sky?" she asked hastily, diverting the conversation to Saúl's favorite topic, and Saúl's steely eyes went briefly soft.

"Excellent footwork as ever. Favors his left, always fights like he's trying to protect someone beside him even when there's nobody beside him, but still the most promising Specialist Alfea has ever seen. I'm not being biased." His eyes bored into Farah, daring her to say he was prejudiced in Sky's favor.

Farah smiled. "Never."

"These are just the facts. Puts in the work as well as having the talent, which is crucial," Saúl continued in his stern voice that was secretly happy. "Wants to room with that boy Riven again next year. I was against it at first, but I'm coming around. The boy's making leaps and bounds at training lately. Choked Mikey half to death at practice this morning."

"Oh good, I love throttled students in the morning," said Farah.

Silva, immune to sarcasm when focused, only nodded with his brows drawn together in thought. "I was thinking of someone different for Sky's partner in battle, someone with a real commitment to the fight, but . . . maybe I was wrong. We don't want the children to grow up exactly like us."

Farah shuddered. "Anything but that."

"Bit worried about Stella," Saúl offered cautiously.

Farah remembered watching the students' faces one by one as she gave the closing address on Orientation Day. Stella, shining the way her light decorations did. Stella's little scheme had been misguided, but Farah had noted the way her magic adorned the school and not just herself. Queen Luna regarded the whole world as a case to show off the jewel that was her flawless self, but Stella—dramatic though she was, flawed though she might be—Farah was certain Stella was different.

Yet Stella being different wouldn't save her. Farah had known people made of heroic stuff before. The stronger the emotion, the stronger the magic, people said, and those who felt most intensely and passionately, those whose light burned the brightest, were at risk of burning out and falling into profound darkness. Rosalind had been powerful and inspiring, a leader Farah had wanted to follow her whole life. Andreas had been a brave, handsome warrior who women had sighed for and dreamed of. And it had all ended in ashes.

"I'm worried about Stella, too," Farah agreed. "The queen is our ally, and I won't speak against her, but it must be difficult to be her child."

Silva obediently didn't speak, but his expression spoke volumes. He had carried out missions for Queen Luna, had been at the palace far more frequently than Farah herself. That was how Sky and Stella had met.

Years ago, Farah had wanted to hide at Alfea and heal. Queen Luna had agreed that she would help cover up the tragedy of Aster Dell. Farah could have Alfea, and Luna would have Farah and Silva's support. It had seemed a fair bargain at the time.

Later, less so. Farah couldn't forget the haunted look in Stella's eyes as she sat in this very office with her hands in fists, begging Farah *not* to help her.

What would a woman who would do this to her own child do to a realm? What *had* Luna done to their realm?

If Luna was a threat to Solaria, Farah would have to act, as she'd acted against Rosalind. But surely, Farah's fears were unfounded. Surely, there could never be another Rosalind, or another Aster Dell.

Farah was so weary at the thought of another battle. She leaned in toward Silva's chair. It was such a relief to speak freely with someone she trusted. "Did you see the way that light burned through the air, as though Stella's magic became another sun for a moment? We can only be thankful that nobody looked directly at it."

Silva's face was intent. "But you can help her."

"I could if she would let me," sighed Farah. "But she won't. She doesn't trust me." She drew in a deep breath. It was bitter to admit, but this was the truth: "None of them ever do. I have never been the approachable type, the type children can come to with their problems. It is my failing, and not my students'. I do not know the trick of charming people to my side, as Rosalind once did. I wish more than anything that I did know it."

Rosalind had owned so much power, but that was the only one Farah envied. She could help the students, if they would only turn to her.

Silva's brows were knit. "If the princess upset you . . ."

"She didn't, of course." Farah made herself smile. "I only wish I knew how to help her better. She has such potential. I spotted several more students with potential at the Orientation Day. I think we're in for an interesting year, next year. Er—was a boy almost drowned down in one of the Specialists' lakes, or is that a strange rumor?"

"It's a beautiful fact." Silva beamed with pride. "Little Terra did it."

Farah was somewhat alarmed. "She did what? Does Ben know?"

Silva shook his head. "Seemed like it would upset him, Farah. No sense in upsetting him, you must see that."

"I feel like someone should address the situation."

"I did address the situation," Silva announced. "I told the Specialist in question that if he bothered any more students, I'd have Terra drown him the rest of the way and then personally weigh down his body in the water so it was never found. Situation handled."

Farah doubted he'd brought up the situation to Terra. She knew Saúl would die for Ben's children. She also knew he would prefer never to have any conversations with them.

He had been a quiet boy, but he was a silent man. The secret he could never tell Sky seemed to have closed his lips to all the world, and Farah respected him too much to ever pry into his mind. She was sometimes afraid that if she did, she would see how much Saúl had lost because of her, and how much he resented her because of it.

It was her fault, and not Saúl's. She was the one who had given the order to stand against Rosalind. Trying to save her and Ben from committing their great sin, Saúl had sacrificed his best friend. Now he had to live with guilt that truly belonged to her. She could never make it up to him.

"Very well, Saúl," she said. "But if Terra tries to duck anyone else with pond weed, or strangle them with vines, or impale them with thorns, I'm having a word with her."

She had received several distressing reports from the gardeners. Terra Harvey's first year of school might prove dangerous, but if Alfea could handle Princess Stella, it could handle Terra as well. It wasn't as if the pair were likely to join forces.

Weeds could crack through stone. Perhaps Terra the force of nature should room with a girl who needed a break-through. Farah recalled the shut-up, desperately reserved face of Musa, the Mind Fairy she'd seen at Orientation Day. That was worth consideration.

Saúl's face indicated he thought Farah's anti-murder rules were cruel and unfair.

"I think Terra should be allowed to throttle Riven with vines if she wants to," he said. "As a treat. Be good for the boy."

"I disapprove of throttling any students, no matter how irritating you find them," said Farah. "I'm taking a stand on this one. If Sky has taken Riven under his wing, I'm sure Riven will turn out all right."

Silva's face lit at the mention of Sky's name, as though the sun had risen over grim granite mountains.

"Perhaps all the students in Alfea will turn out all right," Farah continued. "Perhaps we made all possible mistakes, so there are no mistakes left for our students."

She spoke with more hope than actual belief. She wasn't like Ben, who dreamed he could keep his children safe. But she wasn't like Saúl, either, wanting the children to prepare for war.

What she dreamed of, for all the souls in Alfea, was a space to learn, and grow, and choose. She loved this place because it was where possibilities were born. Possibilities for good, or for evil.

Against her will, Farah's eyes lingered on the space in her office where the secret door was hidden. Then she wrenched her gaze away.

"If any of your students turned out like you," said Silva, "I don't think it would be so bad. The world needs leaders."

Farah hardly knew what to say, she was so touched. "I suppose it does."

Silva stared at his boots. "I don't want the kids to go through what we went through."

All she could do was offer her old friend support. It wasn't much.

"I know what you suffered," Farah said. "I know about the nightmares. You don't have to talk about it, Saúl."

"But . . . it wasn't all nightmares. It wasn't all bad. There are things life gave me that I want my boy to have, too."

Farah gave him a look of inquiry.

"The most important defense a soldier can have is someone you can always trust."

"You still miss Andreas," Farah murmured.

It was only natural. As long as they were both alive,

Andreas and Silva had never been far from each other's side. There was a time when Farah had wished for a little more distance between them, though she loved them both, but now her heart only ached with the pity of it, for the shield-mate left alone.

She was startled when Silva moved, leaning forward.

"Farah," said Silva. There was that softer look in his eyes that usually only happened when he was speaking of Sky. "Not Andreas. I was talking about you."

He reached out and took her hand. Farah looked at their joined hands and remembered finding out that Rosalind had lied, that Aster Dell was not a place of monsters but a village. Farah had been so scared, knowing that she would have to defy their brilliant leader, and fearing she would have to do it alone.

On a single word, Saúl had closed his fingers around the hilt of his sword, ready to fight for her.

"Oh," said Farah, not entirely trusting her own voice, then took a chance. "Saúl, I always wondered. It's almost sixteen years since Aster Dell. If there were children in that village, and if they had lived, they would be almost old enough to come to Alfea by this time. If I don't ask now, I never will."

Silva flinched at the name Aster Dell, but he was listening.

"If we were to go back again, and be faced with the same

choice, and I asked you to follow me all over again. Even knowing what would happen . . . what would you say?"

Silva's eyes stayed on her face another moment, blue as an unwavering candle flame. Then he bowed his head over her hand, as though he might kiss it.

"I would say, 'As you command.'"

They were both reserved individuals. It took approximately three minutes before extreme embarrassment set in.

Silva dropped her hand and got hurriedly to his feet with none of his usual soldier's grace. "I should go . . . check on the . . . weapons."

Farah nodded with conviction. The armory was Saúl's safe space.

"See you tomorrow, Headmaster Silva," she said briskly. "I'm sure it will be another wonderful day of shaping young minds."

Saúl glanced over his shoulder. "Don't know about that. I'm just planning to beat the kids with sticks."

That surprised a laugh out of Farah. Her laugh made Saúl toss her a grin as he left, mischievous and pleased as the boy he'd been once.

Saúl always said how like Andreas Sky was. But when disaster struck, Farah had flown to Saúl like one of Saúl's arrows to a bull's-eye. She would never have chosen Andreas to turn to. There was no question, in Farah's mind, who was the better man. If Sky had the rare courage to stand against a friend, to draw a sword and break his own heart, Farah knew where Sky had learned it.

The door closed behind him, and the headmistress of Alfea was alone in her domain.

Long ago, in the ashes of Aster Dell, Farah had knelt and thought, *I must atone for this. I must make something beautiful.*

She thought of the way Alfea had shimmered on Orientation Day, dusted with starlight by Stella, and once again remembered speaking in front of that gathering of students. Every one a great possibility. In every face, a light.

Perhaps in Alfea there was possibility waiting, even for Farah. Perhaps one day there would be a student who saw past all Farah's reserve, the barriers she'd built against guilt and pain, barriers she knew no way to dismantle now. A fairy who would believe that Farah only wanted to help, and who would trust her to do so. She didn't blame any of the students for not believing in her, but she would give a lot for that. For even one student who would reach out a hand.

It was a strange fancy, but sometimes she thought that if just one student believed in her, perhaps Farah could believe in herself, too. The way she used to when she was young.

She thought of Stella's delicate profile, turning away. Then she thought of Terra, strong as spring, and Aisha, relentless as a current, and Musa, who isolated herself but who'd come to Alfea, anyway. And suddenly, most strangely, Farah thought of that girl Bloom in the human world, with her hair like a flame and her voice like a bell.

Farah set down her empty glass, rose, and shook her head to clear it of visions.

Maybe next year.

She should get back to the paperwork before it grew into a tower and defeated her. Farah had once had a system for dealing with the paperwork, but she'd forgotten crucial parts of it and was now simply attempting to hold back the paper flood.

For a moment, she allowed herself an indulgence and stood at her window, circles upon circles of stained glass flooded by moonlight. The wide ribbon of a river, snaking by the side of manicured lawns. The maze to get lost in and the winged statues commemorating the flight they had lost. The jagged circle of stones, the roaring waterfall, the looming trees, and the tall gray towers of the fairy realm. The depth of the woods and the height of the mountains, and all the grace and guilt and passion and faith of those who lived within these walls.

She could see the castle and its grounds in a dozen different colors, and loved Alfea in every light.

One dream of her youth, the last dream, had come true. Farah Dowling looked out upon the land, and believed she had made something beautiful.

As long as she lived, the dream of Alfea lived, too. And if she was wise and lucky, if she taught her students the best way she knew how, the dream of Alfea might live on. Even after her own death.

FIRE

Bloom Peters, who was magic without knowing it, sat back and sighed in satisfaction as she admired her handiwork. She'd stayed up all night fixing the broken lamp her mother had given her, and it had been worth it. It felt amazing to rescue something beautiful from the wreckage of the past.

The lamp gleamed now, both metal and stained glass, like a flower made of jewels. Yesterday Bloom had found it at her threshold, picked it up, carried it inside, and got to work. She'd felt tempted, when she first saw the lamp, to run down and talk to her mother—but Bloom was always a girl of action.

Now that she wasn't utterly focused on her task, thought crept back in, unwelcome as a draft under her door.

She couldn't believe her mom had come upstairs yesterday, to uneasily mention fires. Bloom knew she was an outcast, but that was a long way from being a criminal.

Bloom wasn't actually sorry the fires had happened. The guy who owned the antiques store was a jerk who'd cheated a grieving woman out of her heirlooms, and the fire in the science lab had started at a bully's desk, a guy who'd made three other students run out of the lab crying last week alone. So what if their stuff had caught fire? Nobody had been hurt. No harm done, except to the property of jerks.

She wasn't sorry, but that was a long way from being the culprit. The way her mom had talked about the fires, the way her mom had looked at her—she hadn't said anything, but it was almost as if her mom believed Bloom had something to do with starting the fires.

Imagine thinking something like that about your own daughter.

Bloom hadn't been anywhere near the fires when they happened, hadn't had any fire-starting materials, and besides, she wasn't a deranged arsonist. If you asked Bloom, the fires were cosmic justice. Bloom got angry with her mother whenever she thought about the implied accusation. She felt fury at her mom's injustice curling and rising hot in her belly, but then reason returned and quenched Bloom's temper.

There might be a distance between them lately, but her mom couldn't *really* believe she would do something like that. It wasn't possible. Bloom wasn't a destroyer. She was a mender of broken things.

Her mom knew that, she was sure. That was why she'd left Bloom the lamp, to show her she hadn't meant it.

Bloom flipped on some music and waved the lamp around, as if it was a baton and she was conducting an orchestra, filled with the joy of success. She would've called up a friend to tell them about it, but she didn't . . . actually have any friends.

People kept their distance from Bloom. They always had. Even her mom had started to drift further and further away from her. Bloom wasn't sure why. She wasn't trying to push anyone away. She didn't *feel* different on the inside, but she guessed she didn't know how other people felt on the inside.

There were many colors in the stained glass of the lampshade, but Bloom's favorite color stood out to her. The crimson stained glass was such a nice red, the color of Dad's good wine, and in a pretty shape. Like wings.

The lamp had come out really nicely. She wanted to show it to her mom, but her mom had stopped being impressed when Bloom fixed things a long time ago, and now she only nagged about mother-daughter yoga classes. When Bloom failed to make friends there, it would be mother-daughter cooking classes, maybe mother-daughter snorkeling. When Bloom was a little kid they used to hang out, just her mom and her, reading books of fairy tales and making up their own dances and fixing broken toys together. She used to be enough for her mom, even if she'd never been the cheerleader type.

Well. Bloom was a little old for fairy tales now.

Bloom had located an abandoned warehouse nearby, where she stored some of the things she salvaged so Mom wouldn't realize how often she did it or how much stuff she actually had. She knew her mom wouldn't want more reminders that Bloom was always tinkering with things instead of joining the cheerleading squad.

Even though her mom obviously knew about the lamp, Bloom was tempted to bring the lamp to the warehouse so she could gloat over her hoard, like a fire-breathing dragon with gold. Maybe Bloom would. She could keep the lamp safe there.

She hummed to herself, cheer renewed, and held up the lamp to the light. If she stared through the stained glass, it turned her boring suburb outside the window crimson and saffron colors, into a whole other world.

Bloom hadn't thought much about college yet, but suddenly she imagined this lamp in a dorm room, where she'd brought it from far away. If she was missing home wherever she ended up, she could look at the lamp and think: *I made this. My mother gave this to me. I carried this light with me from home.*

She'd been drawn to things of the past all her life, but perhaps now it was time to start thinking of the future. Her parents always said Bloom was meant for great things. That sounded good, but it was vague, the kind of thing parents just said. Like, "Believe in yourself, and you can achieve anything." Didn't matter how much Bloom believed in herself, she was unlikely to save a country or become a heroine in a fairy tale. But she could do something, surely. She did want a grand adventure, wanted to prove to her parents that their strange daughter was capable of great things.

She wanted to make her mom proud.

She shoved the fires out of her mind. Mom had left this lamp at Bloom's door as an apology and a gesture of trust. Bloom held the lamp and rested her cheek against the stained glass, the same way she used to rest her cheek against her mother's when she was little and Mom used to swing her up and hold her close.

Sometimes Bloom wished she could make a huge discovery, find a treasure she couldn't even imagine, that was terribly broken. Then Bloom would have the chance to fix it, to make a great wrong right.

California sunlight streamed through her window and lit the ruby wings so they burned scarlet as a flame.

DO MOST BITTER WRONG

Dear Sir,

What did I tell you? Never send an idiot to do a woman's job. I took the opportunity of visiting Alfea on their Orientation Day, and Callum Hunter has proven himself laughably incompetent as our spy. I watched in disbelief as only luck saved him from being exposed when he executed his clumsy maneuvers with truth potion. Callum Hunter won't be able to attract anyone new to our side. That bungler will only drive them away.

I am old enough now. I can go to Alfea myself. I can help you. I can save Rosalind and find a path to the power we need. All the realms will be ours. Every drop of your blood shed will cost our enemies a river. Everything Farah Dowling, Saul Silva, and Ben Harvey cherish, we can take away.

I think I've already spotted a couple of students who might be amenable to joining our side. Trust me to recruit some likely looking boys.

I'll make you proud, Andreas. I'll make you glad you took me in. I promise you, we will have revenge for their treachery, including your so-called best friend's attempt to murder you. The old sins of the traitors in Alfea will finally be paid for. In full.

They sit smug in their castle now, but the final glory will be yours and mine. I swear it on the ashes of Aster Dell.

yours always,
Beatrix

Acknowledgments

Many thanks to Beth Dunfey, my fabulous and understanding editor who always invites me to fun places—this time fairyland! And to Naomi Duttweiler and the whole amazing team at Scholastic.

My deep gratitude always to Suzie Townsend, my glorious agent; the always-on-it Dani Segelbaum; and the wonderful team at New Leaf!

Many thanks also to the whole *Fate: The Winx Saga* team, especially Sarah Sagripanti who had such a good suggestion for Aisha. And to Abigail Cowen—I've never had someone in mind for five books before!—thanks for rocking it as a fairy heroine and a witch, too.

Also a squillion thanks to my Readers in Lockdown, Susan Connolly, who always likes the same bits I do, and Holly Black, who always knew she'd lure me to fairies one day. And those who supported me through Zoom, especially Chiara Popplewell who sent cupcakes.

And to you always, Reader, for reading my fairy tales.